AND THE FATHER IS...

There's been speculation for months surrounding the unnamed father of Brooke Garrison's love child. Well, a source close to the Garrison family revealed exclusively to us that the father is none other than (drumroll, please...) Jordan Jefferies. That's right! The multimillionaire investor and, more importantly, Garrison-family rival, got cozy with the high-society brunette last summer. Our insider reveals that the pair had not seen each other intimately since that one-time romp and that Brooke has repeatedly declined Jordan's marriage offers.

No word yet on Parker's reaction—Brooke's big brother—when he heard the news. Looks like another scandal is about to erupt for the Garrisons.

Dear Reader,

What a thrill it has been to work on THE GARRISONS with so many of my favorite authors! I'm especially excited to present you with the final book in the series.

Christmas certainly brings to mind family time. And what better way to commemorate the season than with the Garrison clan's expanding. Of course, when the newest family member is Jordan Jefferies, long-time enemy of the Garrisons, there is bound to be trouble. It takes a special couple to cement that relationship, and luckily, Brooke Garrison and Jordan Jefferies are up to the challenge. With a large family myself, I enjoyed the privilege of bringing all the Garrisons and Jefferies together to celebrate the holidays—and, of course, weddings!

Merry Christmas, Happy Hanukkah and Season's Greetings to you all!

Holiday hugs,

Catherine Mann

CATHERINE MANN

THE EXECUTIVE'S SURPRISE BABY

Silhouette®

Desire

Published by Silhouette Books

America's Publisher of Contemporary Romance

To the marvelously talented authors of the first five
Garrison stories: Roxanne St. Claire, Sara Orwig, Anna DePalo, Brenda Jackson and
Emilie Rose. I thoroughly enjoyed working with you all on this project!

And to my critique partner, Joanne Rock.
Many, many thanks for your help that made it possible for me to meet my deadline.
I couldn't have done it without your fabulous insights—and the sugar jolt from
that bag of Jelly Bellies you sent during my final dash to the finish line!

Special thanks and acknowledgment
are given to Catherine Mann for her contribution
to THE GARRISONS miniseries.

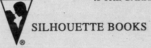 SILHOUETTE BOOKS

ISBN-13: 978-0-373-76837-0
ISBN-10:   0-373-76837-0

THE EXECUTIVE'S SURPRISE BABY

Visit Silhouette Books at www.eHarlequin.com

Printed in U.S.A.

Recent books by Catherine Mann

Silhouette Desire

Baby, I'm Yours #1721
Under the Millionaire's Influence #1787
The Executive's Surprise Baby #1837

Silhouette Romantic Suspense

Private Maneuvers #1226
Strategic Engagement #1257
Joint Forces #1293
Explosive Alliance #1346
The Captive's Return #1388
Awaken to Danger #1401
Fully Engaged #1440
Holiday Heroes #1487
  "Christmas at His Command"

*Wingmen Warriors

CATHERINE MANN

writes contemporary military romances, a natural fit, since she's married to her very own USAF research source. Catherine graduated with a BA in Fine Arts: Theatre from the College of Charleston, and she received her master's degree in Theatre from UNC Greensboro. Now a RITA® Award winner, Catherine finds following her aviator husband around the world with four children, a beagle and a tabby in tow offers her endless inspiration for new plots. Learn more about her work, as well as her adventures in military life, by visiting her Web site: www.catherinemann.com. Or contact her at P.O. Box 41433, Dayton, OH 45441.

THE GARRISONS

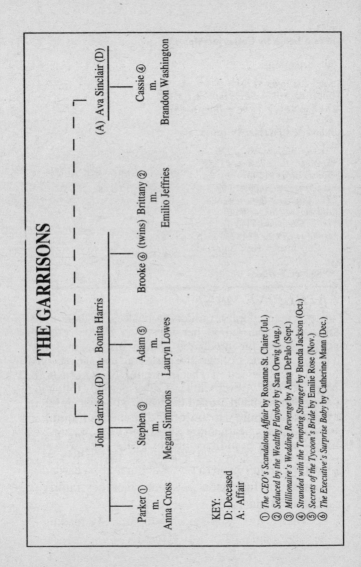

John Garrison (D) m. Bonita Harris ----- (A) Ava Sinclair (D)

Parker ① m. Anna Cross

Stephen ③ m. Megan Simmons

Adam ⑤ m. Lauryn Lowes

Brooke ⑥ (twins) m.

Brittany ② m. Emilio Jeffries

Cassie ④ m. Brandon Washington

KEY:
D: Deceased
A: Affair

① *The CEO's Scandalous Affair* by Roxanne St. Claire (Jul.)
② *Seduced by the Wealthy Playboy* by Sara Orwig (Aug.)
③ *Millionaire's Wedding Revenge* by Anna DePalo (Sept.)
④ *Stranded with the Tempting Stranger* by Brenda Jackson (Oct.)
⑤ *Secrets of the Tycoon's Bride* by Emilie Rose (Nov.)
⑥ *The Executive's Surprise Baby* by Catherine Mann (Dec.)

Prologue

July, five months ago

Brooke Garrison ordered her first taste of alcohol at twenty-eight years old.

She reached across the polished teak wood for the glass of wine from the aging bartender at the Garrison Grand Hotel lounge. Her hand shook after the emotional toll of the day, hearing her father's will read, learning of his secret life. At least she didn't have to worry about getting carded even if she had been younger since her family owned the place.

"Thank you," she said, surreptitiously reading the older man's name tag, "Donald."

"You're welcome, Miss Garrison." He slid an extra napkin her way as smoothly as the pianist slipped into his next song. "And please accept my condolences about your father. He will be missed."

By more people than she had realized. "We all appreciate the kind words. Thank you again."

"Of course. Let me know if you need anything else."

Anything else? She would like to erase this whole horrible day and start over. Or at least stop thinking about it, much less talking. She'd already ignored four voice messages from her brother Parker's receptionist.

Tentatively, Brooke sipped the wine, wincing. She watched the candle's flame through the chardonnay's swirl. Somewhere in that glass were the answers to what stole her mother away from her. To what had driven her father to lead a secret second life in the years before he'd died.

Her alcoholic mother's bitter words after the reading of John Garrison's will this morning echoed over and over again through Brooke's head. "The cheating son of a bitch. I'm glad he's dead."

What a hell of a way to learn there weren't five Garrison offspring—but six. In addition to three brothers and an identical twin sister, Brooke had an illegitimate half sister living in the Bahamas, a sister her father had never told them about while he was alive. Instead, he'd chosen to share the news in his will while handing over a sizable chunk of the Garrison empire to Cassie Sinclair—the newly discovered sibling.

Not that Brooke cared about the money. The betrayal, however, burned.

Conversations and clinking glasses of happier people swelled around her while she sipped. She wanted none of the revelry, even made a point of carefully avoiding eye contact with a couple of men attempting to snag her attention.

Brooke raised the long-stemmed crystal to her mouth again. She knew the wine was as top-notch as the fresh flowers and linens around her. Her taste buds, however, registered nothing. She was too numb with grief.

She'd always blamed her mother for her father's frequent business trips. The drinking must have driven her wonderful daddy away. Now she couldn't help but wonder if her father's behavior had somehow contributed to her mother's unhappiness.

And how could she untangle it all in the middle of mourning the loss of such a huge figure in her life? The hotel blared reminders of his presence. She could see her father's imprint on each multi-domed chandelier in the bar, on every towering column.

Brooke circled a finger around the top of her half-full glass, an indulgence she never allowed herself because of her mother's addiction.

Tonight wasn't normal.

Her eyes hooked on the looming columns in the spacious hall outside the bar—the evening turning further beyond *normal* than she ever could have anticipated.

Through the arched entranceway walked the last man she expected here, but one she recognized well even in the dim lighting. Their families had been business rivals for years, a competition that only seemed to increase once Jordan Jefferies had taken over after his father's death.

So why was Jordan here now?

Brooke forced herself to think more like her siblings and less like her peacemaker self…and the obvious answer came to her. He'd come to her brother Stephen's hotel to scope out the competition.

Brooke took the unobserved moment to study Jordan Jefferies prowling the room with a lion's lazy grace. No, wait. Lazy was the wrong word.

Think like her siblings. Jefferies would only want people to perceive a lazy lope so he could pounce while she was otherwise occupied staring at his blond, muscle-bound good looks.

Yeah, she'd noticed his looks more than once. He might be the enemy, but she wasn't blind. However, she'd considered him off-limits because of the controversy it would cause in her family. Often, she'd heard her oldest brother Parker fume for days over a contentious business meeting with Jordan. The family diplomat, she always tried her best to soothe over arguments and hurt feelings.

For all the good it had done her. The whole Garrison clan had been ripped raw today.

Her mother's voice whispered again... "The cheating son of a bitch. I'm glad he's dead."

The bartender swooped by, breaking her train of thought. "Can I get you anything else, Miss Garrison?"

Garrison. She couldn't escape it anywhere around here, just as futile as thinking she could keep peace in her family.

Why bother trying?

A heat fired through her veins and bloomed into an idea, a desire. And sure, a need for open rebellion after a day of hell. "Yes, Donald, actually you can do something for me. Please tell the gentleman over there—" she pointed to Jordan "—that his drinks for the evening are on the house."

"Of course, Miss Garrison." The bartender smiled discreetly and walked under the rows of hanging glasses to the other side of the wooden bar. He leaned to relay the message and Brooke waited. Her stomach tightened in anticipation.

What would he think of her picking up the tab for his drinks? Likely nothing more than a Garrison acknowledging his presence.

Would Jordan Jefferies even remember her? Of course he would. He was a savvy businessman who would know all the Garrisons. A better question, would he be able to tell her apart from her twin?

He looked from the bartender to her. His gaze met hers, and even in the low lighting she could see the blue of his eyes. Interest sparked in his slow smile.

Jordan picked up his drink and wove his way around the patrons, straight toward her with a deliberate, unhesitating pace. He set his glass beside hers. "I didn't expect such a nice welcome from a Garrison. Are you sure you didn't have the bartender poison my drink, Brooke?"

He recognized her. Or a lucky guess?

"How do you know I'm not Brittany?"

Without ever glancing away from her eyes, he reached, stopping an inch shy of touching a lock of her hair that stubbornly refused to stay pulled back. "Because of this. That wayward strand is signature Brooke."

Wow. He definitely recognized *her* when even her own father had gotten it wrong sometimes.

In that moment, she realized she had more Garrison determination in her than anyone would have ever suspected. Brooke lifted her glass to Jordan in a silent toast.

She'd seen him many times. She'd always wanted him.

Tonight, her family be damned, she would have him.

One

"**M**erry Christmas, I'm having a baby. Your baby," Brooke Garrison corrected the phrasing, wanting to get it just right before the father of her child walked through her office door.

Any second now.

She shifted behind her sleek metal desk from where she managed the family's Sands Condominium Development. She toyed with her hair. Longed for more peppermint ice cream—yes, she'd eaten a scoop with breakfast.

Damn. Time was ticking away faster than the blinking lights on the Christmas tree in the corner of her office, and she still didn't know the perfect way to tell Jordan about his impending fatherhood.

"I'm pregnant, and it's yours." She practiced another tact. "The birth control we used apparently failed. Probably when we were in the hot tub."

Hmm… She shook her head. Bad idea thinking about sharing a bath with Jordan. She swiped back a lock of hair that had slithered free from her French twist. As manager of Sands Condominium Development—a segment of the Garrison family empire—she should be more decisive than this.

Except nothing had ever been more important.

"I'm expecting." Expecting what? That sounded like FedEx should be showing up soon with a package. She kicked off her heels that had long ago started pinching her swollen feet, even without panty hose.

Thanks to her ever-present tan, a by-product of living in Miami's South Beach, she could go without stockings. And why was she thinking about clothing accessories?

Likely to avoid the subject that jangled her nerves.

She should have already prepared the flawless speech. The Garrison family perfectionist, never making waves, she was always organized. Not so much now.

Worst of all, there was no excuse for her lack of prep work. Once she'd dropped the pregnancy news bomb at the weekly family dinner, she'd known it was only a matter of time until word got out. Eventually her future brother-in-law, Emilio, would un-wittingly say something to his own brother—and business partner.

Jordan Jefferies.

When her secretary had buzzed her with the news that her family's biggest business rival would like to see her, Brooke had known that *eventually* had arrived.

Sooooo, what about, "Remember that night five months ago after they read my father's will? When I actually indulged in three sips of wine?" Dumb move having any at all since she never drank for fear of being like her alcoholic mother. "And after that, we had wild monkey sex in a hotel room until—"

The door opened and her mouth closed.

Jordan didn't fling it wide or send it crashing against the wall. He didn't need to. The man in a gray pin-striped suit had the kind of presence that resonated through a room more than any echo of wood pounding wall. The diamond cuff links and tailored perfection of him contrasted with her memories of their raw, heated night together.

Six feet three inches tall, he nearly skimmed the mistletoe dangling from her door frame. As quietly as he entered, he closed the door behind him.

The lock snicked. She flinched. His baby kicked.

Jordan turned to face her and strode toward her desk, his handsome face an unreadable mask. As she took in his perfect blond hair, she resented her stubborn strand that wouldn't stay in place. He knelt briefly and straightened, coming back up with her shoes. A whiff of his aftershave drifted across the steel desk, sending her back to the morning she'd hugged a hotel pillow to inhale the scent of him. Before she'd left him sleeping.

"Hello, Brooke." He placed one shoe on her desk, but kept the other black leather pump cupped in his hand. "Don't bother getting up on my account."

"Since you have my shoes, I believe I'll keep my seat." And camouflage her burgeoning stomach behind the office furniture for a few more minutes. A technicality, sure, but it offered a semblance of control.

At least he wasn't shouting, but then he'd had time to absorb the news about her pregnancy. She just needed to be sure he knew—believed—the child was his.

An odd thought struck her. Could she have used telling the family—in front of his adopted brother—as a passive-aggressive way of getting the news to Jordan? While she considered herself a savvy businesswoman who earned her place in the family corporation, she had a reputation for avoiding all-out confrontations in her personal life.

Had she dodged a bullet? Or merely made matters worse? She tried to get a read off Jordan's expression, but he kept her shuttered out with his best executive poker face.

His thumb caressed the leather shoe—and, my, how she hated the way that simple gesture had her curling her toes against a shiver of longing for his hands on her again. It must be hormones. She'd read in one of the pregnancy books that the middle trimester brought an extra surge of sensuality, something she hadn't believed until this moment.

"I'm pregnant," she blurted. So much for a dignified speech. Definitely not a time to add Merry Christmas.

"So I hear." His blue eyes heated over her, unblinking.

"And it's yours."

"Of course."

Arrogant, *sexy* ass. All wishes to avoid confrontation slipped away as something unusually contrary snapped inside her. But then she never acted as expected around this man. "Why are you so sure?"

"Because you told me." He walked around the edge of the desk and set her shoe on the mouse pad. "I've doubled my father's fortune by knowing who to trust and who's a liar."

"You're awfully sure of yourself."

"I've never been wrong before, Brooke. I'm assuming it was during the hot tub. We got a little carried away then." His silky blue eyes oozed sensuality at just the mere mention of that steamy encounter.

She gulped. "Uh-huh. That would be my guess."

He tucked her wayward hair behind her ear. "Besides, your soulful brown eyes aren't a liar's eyes."

She forced her gaze to stay firmly locked with his—while vice-gripping the edge of the desk so her chair wouldn't roll back. She wasn't ready to reveal her stomach, to be that vulnerable. Not yet. "You're saying I'm a sap?"

"I'm saying you're a good person. Far more so than I am, actually." His hand fell to the leather blotter she'd cleared of paperwork for this meeting. "Besides, what would you gain by telling me this? Nothing."

"Ah, so your belief in me has more to do with logic than any mystical eye-reading abilities."

"Brooke. Quit stalling."

Babbling Brooke. Her father used to call her that whenever she got nervous. Yet she'd worked so hard to cultivate a cool facade after years of her mother's hurtful, drunken jibes.

Jordan was right. She was stalling, and all because she suffered from a silly, ridiculous—shallow—moment of self-consciousness. She definitely didn't look like the same woman who'd crawled into bed with Jordan five months ago. Why couldn't he have stayed on the other side of the desk for this conversation?

So much for vanity.

She rolled her chair back across the rose-colored Persian carpet and presented him with an unfettered view of her green dress clinging to her pregnant belly.

Holy hell. Jordan's mouth dried up.

He'd heard about the *pregnancy glow* from friends and workmates, and quite frankly had thought it to be pure bunk. Until now.

Brooke's creamy skin had a touch-me luster. Her

silky brown hair glistened with an extra sheen he could swear had multiplied since he'd last seen her.

And the new swell of her breasts… His hands itched to explore them all over again.

Finally, he let his gaze land on the curve of her stomach where the baby grew. Now *that* stirred something else altogether inside him. Something primal.

His child.

He'd known from the moment he heard the due date that the child was his. However, seeing the proof here in front him, seeing Brooke so amazingly full of his baby… He felt an all-new connection to her and to the life they'd created together. He wasn't going to be shuffled aside, especially not by any stubborn Garrison with her fortress of family support.

Jordan corralled his thoughts and narrowed his focus to her chin with that signature Garrison cleft. People might call him the hard-ass in the boardroom when it came to dealings for Jefferies Brothers, Incorporated, but he decided it wouldn't hurt to let her see how this moment had rocked him.

He sat on the edge of her desk and exhaled long, hard. "Damn, Brooke, that's amazing."

Her gorgeous smile told him he'd struck gold.

Her hand fell to rest over the slight curve. "I'm still getting used to it myself. That's why I haven't gotten around to telling you, yet."

He figured it wouldn't be prudent to mention she'd found time to tell her whole freaking family.

Alienating her gained him nothing and risked everything. "What matters is we're here, now, together."

Together. The word stirred memories of their shared night. Those recollections linked up with the heat surging through him now simply by looking at her, by watching her pupils dilate in response.

Why not let his attraction to Brooke—an attraction that had full well been reciprocated by her— be turned to his advantage?

He reached again to stroke a stray lock back from her face. He took a slow moment to test the feel of it between his fingers, then graze her cheek with his knuckles, her skin as soft as her hair.

"Jordan," she began, her brow furrowing in a surefire precursor to a discussion he hoped to forestall. "I know this could get complicated, but I'll have my lawyers contact yours about making sure you have—"

He dipped his head to capture her next word with his mouth. She tasted like peppermint and temptation.

The peppermint was new. The latter part, he remembered from that fateful night five months ago when they'd crossed paths in the Garrison Grand. He'd been scoping out the competition as he worked on building his Hotel Victoria.

Sure he'd seen her before, but there had been something about her that night, something vulnerable that had called to him. Before he could say bad decision, they'd been making out in an elevator on their way up to a room.

Lips and tongues meeting pretty much the way they were now. Yes, he definitely remembered that, as well as the graceful line of her back under his hands. The feel of her fingers gripping his shoulders. All of it stirred him again with a surprising jolt.

He couldn't afford to lose control. He needed to corral his thoughts with so much at stake with their child, not to mention the business implications of a family merger with a Garrison.

Jordan eased his mouth from hers and tucked her head against his chest as he worked to slow his heart rate. The gusts of her breaths along his neck told him she was every bit as affected by him—which didn't help calm him.

Still, his hands smoothed along her back. The timing to woo her over would be tough for him with the preparations for opening his Hotel Victoria next month, a smaller hotel than her family's Garrison Grand. But he was certain it would rival the Garrison property in luxury—and attract the same clientele. Hell, yes, he'd earned his ruthless business reputation honestly.

He would need that same drive now to win her over. Not only because of the baby, but also because he knew the chemistry he and Brooke shared didn't come around all that often. In fact, he couldn't think of any other woman who turned him inside out with the stroke of her hand the way she could, not even the ex-Playboy bunny he'd dated—and broken up with shortly before that steamy night with Brooke.

Jordan nuzzled her ear. "No lawyers." He nipped the lobe, tugging on her diamond earring gently. "A judge. Two rings." His hand slid around to cup the sweet fullness of her. "And a bouquet by the end of the week, because this child will be born to married parents."

Two

Marry him?

Was he out of his flipping mind?

Or maybe she'd lost hers. Brooke pulled out of his arms so she could regain her balance in the rolling chair. Certainly Jordan's kisses had a powerful effect over her, a large part of why she'd run from his bed so hard and fast five months ago.

The utter loss of control she'd felt with him scared the spit out of her, then and now. "Marry you?"

"Of course." He stroked two fingers down the length of her ever-errant stray lock of hair until she thought maybe she would leave her hair that way from now on. "It makes perfect sense. You're carrying my kid. Our families have been feuding long enough, don't you think? That sort of contentious environment can't be good for a child. Now that Emilio is engaged to Brittany, the rift has started to mend. We can solidify that by marrying each other and fully merging the two family corporations."

Wow, he'd almost had her thinking he possessed a heart, right up to the last word…*corporations*. She pushed out of her chair and stalked away from him, toward the Christmas tree, pivoting back with a huff. "Shall I give you a club to go with your caveman orders?"

"You want romance?" His blue eyes narrowed, then turned heavy lidded, sexy. "I can give you romance. I simply thought a practical woman like you would appreciate the no-nonsense approach to business dealings."

"Whoa. Back up there, Mr. Romeo Incorporated. You romanced me more than enough five months ago, thanks all the same."

Jordan's heat seared her now, as well. "Then answer my question."

She couldn't regret that night because she refused to let her baby ever feel like a mistake. And the sex had been beyond amazing, but good heavens, she wouldn't enter a marriage based on attraction and business mergers. She also refused to risk a sham of a marriage like her parents lived.

"No." She crossed her arms under her breasts. "I will not marry you."

His jaw flexed.

"Be reasonable, Jordan. We barely know each other."

"We've known each other for years."

"As business acquaintances who've sat in a large meeting maybe three times or passed each other in the same restaurant on occasion." Strange how memorable each of those encounters seemed. She'd always noticed him, but placed him in the off-limits category.

Until that night.

That night when Brooke had been mourning the loss of her father. The loss of an image. She'd always been Daddy's girl, running to him when her drunken mother's barbs were too much to bear. To find that her father had lied to them all, as well…

She couldn't think of that now. She had her own child to consider. Providing a stable home for her baby had to come before some illogical desire to lose herself in another kiss from Jordan.

He scooped up one of her shoes and tapped the heel against her mouse pad. "Yet suddenly you've decided to avoid me."

"Because I wasn't ready to tell you about the baby." She decided he didn't need the extra ammo of knowing why she'd run scared from his naked side.

"Or because the fireworks between us were too much for you to handle."

Apparently he was more intuitive than she'd given him credit for.

"The same could be said for you." Okay, so perhaps her pride stung at the fact he hadn't gone out of his way to pursue her.

"I called you."

"A week later." There went her pride again.

He set her shoe down, his eyes narrowing with a predatory gleam. "You tell me to stay away, and I'm supposed to ignore what you say? Does that mean when you say you won't marry me, I'm supposed to ignore that, too?"

He was a wily one. No wonder her oldest brother said Jordan made such a fearsome adversary in the boardroom. Which brought up yet another complication since the baby's father just happened to want a toehold in her family's company. Marrying her would give him that connection to the Garrison business he'd always craved.

God, she hated the path her mind was taking. But damn it, he was the one who'd said they could merge corporations. If that didn't give a woman the right to be leery, she didn't know what would.

"Don't be obtuse, Jordan. I won't marry you. We don't know anything important about each other as people, anything outside the bedroom." Don't go there with the thoughts. "To base a marriage on a brittle foundation of sex and mutual business interests would be catastrophic and horribly unfair to our child."

"All right then." He smiled—wow, how he smiled. He shoved away from the desk and strode toward her. "Let's get to know each other better.

For our child. We're going to be linked by this kid for the rest of our lives. It's the Christmas season. Let's celebrate and use this time to build a stronger foundation."

"That sounds logical." If she knew him better, then she could better judge his motivations for wanting to be a part of her life as well as the baby's.

"Good, good." He nodded as he walked by her, past the Christmas tree.

No kiss? No more trying to persuade her to marry him? That was it?

"Jordan?"

She eyed him warily as he strode toward the door, paused and glanced back over his shoulder.

"I'll pick you up at eight tonight for our date." The door clicked closed behind him.

Date?

She'd thought they were going to get to know each other, as in meet at the lawyer's office to draw up visitation agreements, perhaps have coffee afterwards. But dating?

She'd just been royally maneuvered, and she wouldn't give over complete control that easily. Yes, she could see how *dating* would be a good idea, however, she resented the way he assumed she would fall in line with his plans. She didn't want the world to know about them yet, damn it.

Time to show Jordan Jefferies that while she might be the quiet Garrison, she had every bit as much determination as the rest.

When it came to how they would get to know each other, she could make plans of her own.

At six-thirty that evening, Brooke pulled her BMW convertible past a row of palm trees and a hibiscus hedge into the side parking lot of the Hotel Victoria—eight impressive floors of brass and glass set on the South Beach shore.

The construction workers should be gone for the evening. She knew from casual conversations with Emilio that Jordan had opened an office in a completed suite where he could oversee the last stages of finishing the hotel, and he always stayed late. The place was his well-known pet project of Jefferies Brothers, Incorporated's many holdings. So he would undoubtedly want to spend every free moment overseeing the construction.

She'd worn sunglasses in hopes of keeping a low profile. It helped that no one would expect to find a Garrison here. The world could know about her relationship with Jordan when she was good and ready.

Now she just had to get past security.

Brooke flipped open her cell phone and punched in Jordan's private number he'd given her five months ago, a number she'd almost used at least a hundred times. The ringing stopped.

"Jordan?"

"Brooke, you're not backing out."

"Who says I'm breaking the date?" she retorted.

He thought he knew her. She would enjoy surprising him. "I'm downstairs."

"Down where?"

"Outside your place. At the Hotel Victoria. Could you please tell your security guy to let me up?"

His two-beat hesitation offered the only sign she'd shocked him. "I'll be down in less than a minute."

Sure enough, before she could step out of her car, Jordan pushed through the back entrance toward her. She tugged the picnic basket with her and slammed the car door.

His steps faltered briefly, his gaze hooking on her Little Red Riding Hood basket. "I made dinner reservations for eight-thirty."

"I can't wait that long to eat. I'll be starving way before then." She stopped in front of him, the basket between them. "Would you be responsible for depriving your baby of food?"

He brushed his thumb over the dimple in her chin. "What game are you playing here?"

She didn't want to be tempted by his touch, especially when they would be alone for the evening. But going out in public together? She wasn't ready for that yet. "I don't want to go out. I'm tired and my feet hurt. I want to enjoy my dinner and relax without a bunch of curious people watching us, or worse yet, asking questions."

"Fair enough," he conceded. "Let's go inside." He took the basket from her and guided her toward the hotel entrance.

Letting him steer her with the heat of his hand on her waist, she couldn't deny the curiosity itching over her to check out the rival hotel of the Garrison Grand. Inside, she inhaled the scent of fresh paint, undoubtedly soon to be replaced with a more exotic aroma.

No question, this place targeted the same clientele as her family's South Beach property, yet she couldn't help but be struck by the décor contrast. The Garrison Grand stayed with a theme of mostly pristine white, with the richest of wood, marble and steel accents.

The Victoria fired through her in a blast of bold reds and yellow, with brass accents. Cherrywood, marble and decadence were the only decorative themes in common.

Best not to think about marble, though, which could too easily lead her to memories of the marble spa tub they'd once enjoyed.

The brass doors to the elevator swooshed open, and she stepped inside with Jordan—and more memories. Had she made the right decision today? She tried to avoid looking at him, but the mirrored walls made that impossible. "Your hotel is beautiful."

"*You* are beautiful."

"And *you* are not going to get me against the elevator wall that easily again, Romeo."

His low laugh followed her as she walked out of the elevator, then she realized she didn't know where to turn. Jordan touched her elbow and guided her left toward the double doors at the end of the corridor. He swiped his key and she found—not what she'd expected.

Wait. "I was thinking we would eat in your office."

Not in a sitting room that obviously connected to a bedroom.

Control slipped elusively away. She longed to call for a time-out and simply plop to rest on one of the comfy buttercream-yellow and burgundy sofas or seats stationed throughout the lobby. Or better yet, kick off her shoes and take to the beach beyond the glass wall, wade through the aquamarine waters.

"I'm living and working from here now, just until they finish up the last touches to the hotel. Saves time leaving my house for every call." He tugged at the knot in his striped tie and slowly slid the length free from his collar.

At the deliberate, sensuous glide of the silk against his cotton shirt, her stomach flipped and it had nothing to do with an acrobatic baby. "Okay, can I get you something to drink? I brought water, and uh, water. Oh, and milk."

Let him see what life with her would be like. No wild nights at a bar. Of course he could always go to his own minibar and mix himself something to drink. She waited…

He extended a hand. "I'll have the water."

She reached into the basket and pulled free a bottle of sparkling water. She poured it into two crystal glasses with ice from the minibar, topped it off with a twist of lemon before flipping the lid closed on the basket again... To find him in the doorway with his cell phone in hand.

He covered the mouthpiece. "I'm canceling our reservations at Emilio's restaurant. It seems you have dinner well in hand."

Emilio's? Her mouth watered for the amazing Cuban cuisine offered at El Diablo. Being a captive to her hormonal cravings really sucked sometimes. She chewed her bottom lip and stared at the basket of... She couldn't even remember what was inside anymore.

Jordan covered the phone's mouthpiece. "I had this assistant once who was pregnant. She ate cheeseburgers for lunch every day for a month. She vowed nothing else sounded good. You know, we can pitch the stuff in your basket and I can place a delivery order at El Diablo's—for the baby."

She released her lip from between her teeth, slowly. "For the baby?"

"Absolutely."

"Okay." She rattled off her order before her pride could get the better of her, each delicacy filling her taste buds with anticipation.

"Got it." His smile and wink took away some of the sting to her pride at losing a bit of control in her plan.

He relayed her order, doubled to include himself. Finally he closed his phone and ditched his suit coat over the back of a wooden chair, the wide bed visible through the part in the slightly open connecting door.

She took in the framed prints on the walls, each

photo portraying a stage of construction of the hotel. All but one small family photo resting by his computer… She started toward it, curious, but Jordan waylaid her.

He took his glass in one hand and her elbow in his other. "The balcony?"

Since she could swear he'd phrased it as a question rather than an order, she decided to go along. "The balcony, yes."

Lord love him, after she sat, he even thought to swing another wrought-iron chair around to prop her tired feet while they enjoyed the final fading rays of the day. He really was pulling out all the stops.

Sinking back into her seat, she sighed at the amazing view of the waves rolling against the private beach. "You've got a great piece of prime property here."

"Thanks."

She enjoyed the beauty of the sculptured landscaping, empty now, but soon undoubtedly to be flooded with people. "Who needs blood pressure medicine with a mood stabilizer like this?"

His eyebrows drew together. "A lot going on to stress you out lately?"

She rested her hand on her stomach. "I'm excited about the baby, don't get me wrong. But the news certainly frightened me at first." She didn't have much in the way of positive role-modeling for motherhood.

"I wish you would have told me."

"The thought of doing that really sent my heart pounding." She pulled out the pins from her French twist and shook her hair loose in the ocean breeze.

"I'm that scary?"

"I wouldn't say scary, exactly." Intimidating. "Pushy." That sounded nicer.

"You're as diplomatic as the rest of your family," he answered wryly.

Actually, she was usually the family diplomat. "I don't believe you mean that as a compliment."

He stayed silent, his executive face in place as he studied her for a lengthy moment while seagulls scavenged along the talcum-white shore for a late-day snack. "So clue me in to what I have done to warrant such great fear. You don't tell me about our baby for months. After being left out of the loop about my own child, I come to you directly—calmly, I might add."

He had a point. She stared at her feet, guilt pinching as much as her shoes. She kicked off the heels and wiggled her toes. "Uh, I'm sor—"

"Wait, hold that thought. I'm not finished." He held up a hand. "Then I do the heinous, awful thing of proposing marriage. And when you crush my spirit by turning me down, I ask you out on a date." He thumped himself on the forehead. "Damn. I sure am one helluva jackass."

Laughter bubbled inside her. "Okay, okay, you've made your point. You've been more than fair, and I was wrong not to tell you sooner. I apologize, and I really mean it. This is simply something I've needed time to become accustomed to myself, but I'm here with you now. No matter what happens with these dates of ours, you will be a part of our child's life if that's what you want."

"Don't doubt that for a second."

His steely determination sent a shiver up her spine and her arms around her swelling waistline protectively.

"When Emilio told you about my pregnancy, did you let him know about us?"

He shook his head, leaning back in his chair, water glass tapping against his knee. "I wanted to speak with you first." His eyes widened. "So your whole family doesn't know I'm the father yet. Not even your twin. Damn. You're a good secret keeper. I could use someone like you in my company."

"That's why I didn't want to go out tonight. I've kept the baby news under wraps by wearing bulky clothes and staying away from the social scene for the most part, but my stomach has really popped these past couple of weeks. Once you and I are seen out in public together, people will make the logical connection. I need to tell the family about us first."

"Let's do it then. Call a family meeting."

He had to be kidding. He actually wanted to be there when all the Garrisons heard she'd hooked up with Jordan Jefferies? Of course, she would have to inform her family sometime.

"Actually, we all gather every Sunday for dinner so that would be the easiest, most logical time."

"All right, if you think this is the best way. They're your family."

The problem was, there would be no best way to tell them about Jordan Jefferies—the head of her family's rival company. A rivalry that still existed even though somewhat softened since Emilio entered the fold.

She stared up at the stars just beginning to wink at her and willed her heart rate to slow. After all, she needed to keep a level head. She still had a whole weekend of date nights to get through with Jordan before the big family confrontation.

And for now, just making it back out Jordan's door without glancing in the direction of his bed seemed like a Herculean feat.

Three

Guess who's coming to dinner?

The phrase kept clicking through Brooke's head during the drive to her family's estate late Sunday afternoon.

The words only drummed louder as Jordan pulled past the security gates up the brick drive toward the ambling stucco mansion with a red tile roof—her childhood home. She suffered no delusions that this would go smoothly. The boardroom hatred between her family and Jordan was longstanding and deep.

She still could hardly believe they'd accepted Emilio into their family, in spite of his partnership in Jefferies Brothers, Incorporated. It said a lot for how much Brittany loved Emilio. However, there wasn't love present this time, and she feared her family would sense that.

Jordan slid the Jaguar into Park behind the line of other luxury cars. Apparently her siblings had already arrived.

She was lucky to have been born into her family's wealth, and she worked her tail off managing the Sands Condominium Development to prove she deserved it. Still, that hadn't stopped some from labeling her a silver-spoon, trust-fund baby. It also hadn't stopped many two-faced people from wanting something from her. Brooke rubbed the goose bumps along her arms in spite of the temperate Miami December afternoon.

Jordan rounded the hood to open Brooke's door and lead her up the stairs to the massive mahogany and glass double doors. Garland and bows draping the entrance reminded her of a holiday she hadn't found time to begin preparing for.

Before they even made it to the top step, the doors swept open to reveal an older lady in a starched blue dress and white apron. "Good evening, Miss Brooke."

"Hello, Lissette. Could you please let them know in the kitchen that there will be one more for dinner?"

"Of course, Miss Brooke, we'll have yours out directly."

Noise rattled from the dining room, clinking silverware against china. Requests for passing this and that, a normal sounding family dinner.

Little did they know…

Jordan glanced down at Brooke. "Your face is pale. Are you all right? Do you need to sit down? We don't have to do this today. We can keep right on with our apartment dates—"

She squeezed his arm. "I'm fine." Although she had enjoyed their simple dinners at his place and hers. How she wished they could keep it simple, and yes, hidden, for a while longer. "But thank you for worrying."

He winked.

Her heels clicked along the tile floors as she made her way across the foyer past the winding staircase, the click, click echoing up to the cavernous ceiling. A Christmas tree—at least twelve feet tall—twinkled. Perfectly wrapped gifts lay beneath. The decorations were beyond lavish this year since Brittany and Emilio would be celebrating a Christmas wedding in three weeks with the reception held here.

Brooke forced even breaths past her lips. All the more reason to reveal the news now and give the dust time to settle so she wouldn't ruin Brittany's big day.

They stopped in the dining room entry, waiting. She took the unobserved moment to study her family at the table.

Her brother Parker would blow a gasket. Even with the softening influence of his new wife, Anna, her oldest brother was still unrelenting when it came to his business dealings. His dislike—wow, what a way to soft-soap that—for Jordan was common knowledge.

Her brother Adam had always been emotionally distant from all of them, only just beginning to open up since his surprise marriage to the straight-laced Lauryn.

At least Stephen wasn't here. One less angry brother to worry about.

Her gaze skipped over her mother—downing a glass of wine—and settled on those most likely to be her allies. Her outgoing twin, Brittany, sat with fiancé Emilio Jefferies.

Even with Emilio's new standing in the Garrison family, Brooke suffered no delusions. Jordan was the power force behind Jefferies' attempts to one-up Garrison Inc. by any means possible.

A shattering glass silenced the room.

Brooke jolted as all eyes shifted to Bonita, the matriarch. Her wineglass in shards at her feet, Bonita clapped her hand over her mouth and pointed a wavering finger toward the entryway.

Perhaps Brooke should have made this announcement alone after all.

"Mother, everybody, I've brought someone along for dinner. He obviously needs no introduction."

Brittany snorted.

Brooke shot her twin a *you're-not-helping* glare.

Her impish twin crinkled her nose with an unspoken *sorry*.

Brooke nodded briefly before stepping deeper into the room, forcing her tense facial muscles to smile, damn it. Just pretend things were normal. She paused in front of her chair at the table set for seven, ever aware of the looming man at her back. "I realize this is likely a bit of a shock, but for the sake of family unity, I would appreciate it if we could be civil adults and welcome a guest."

She gauged the noiseless diners around the table. Stunned silent? Or quietly accepting? For a woman who didn't do confrontation, she figured she was making a heck of a good show. "We'll all be seeing a lot of each other in the future since…" She swallowed down the lump in her throat and avoided looking at her mother. "Since…"

So much for her bold approach.

Jordan's hand fell to rest on her shoulder. "I'm the father of Brooke's baby."

She glanced back at him in a quick moment of gratitude that he was there to speak the words she found so hard to say.

Bonita moaned and reached for her Bloody Mary resting by her full water glass while a maid still hovered around the broken glass at her feet. Where was she finding all these drinks? Her brothers usually did a better job at keeping them out of her hands. Things were definitely spiraling out of control.

Parker's chair scraped back as he stood. "Brooke, move."

She shook her head. "Not a chance, Parker."

Her brother kept his eyes pinned on his rival. "Damn it, Brooke, I said *move.*"

Jordan's fingers twitched on her shoulder. "Don't speak to her that way."

A vein throbbed in Parker's temple. "Who the hell are you to tell me how to speak to my sister?"

"I'm the man who's going to marry your sister."

Before she could remind Jordan she'd only agreed to date him, he'd gently moved her aside as Parker shouted, "Like hell."

In a blink both men launched across the table.

The candelabra toppled into a crystal serving dish of asparagus. Gasps echoed. Someone yelped. China and silverware clinked and scattered.

She'd seen her brothers scuffle in their younger years, but that had been simple roughhousing. She'd never seen an all-out fight before. An honest-to-God, muscles bulging, men-out-for-blood pounding on each other.

It wasn't pretty. And it wasn't sexy. All the polish of their everyday ways negotiating deals in boardrooms peeled away to reveal the true cutthroat nature that had propelled them to the top. Their rawness scared her as they rolled off the edge of the table onto the floor in a crash of shattering glassware and honed bodies meeting tile.

The women shot to their feet, advanced a step, then backed away. The other two men at the table simply lounged back. What the hell was wrong with them?

Brooke stamped her heel. "Adam, Emilio, step in before one of them breaks something vital."

Her brother and Jordan's lumbered to their feet as if in no big hurry to end the show.

Adam strode past, leaning toward her. "This has been a long time coming between them. Sure you don't want to let them just work it out of their systems for a while longer?"

"Adam!" she warned a second before Parker landed a punch to Jordan's jaw, not that Jordan even flinched. Instead, the father of Brooke's child flipped his rival on his back in a move that slammed them both into the serving cart.

There went dessert.

Emotions swirled through her—guilt over bringing Jordan into this lair without more forewarning. Annoyance at him and Parker for not staying civilized.

And ohmigod, divided loyalties.

Adam sighed. "Okay, okay…"

Her brother, the middle of the Garrison brood, nodded to Emilio for assistance. The two men made their way toward the pair still duking it out.

Bonita whimpered between gulps of her Bloody Mary. "Another Garrison bastard."

Brooke grabbed the edge of the table to steady herself. The last thing she needed right now was condemnation from her mother, even as much as Brooke wanted to defend her child and her illegitimate sister Cassie. Focus on getting the men quieted down first so she could sit and rest her throbbing feet. Her aching heart.

Emilio and Adam dodged flying fists to grab an elbow and haul the two apart, no easy task given the thrashing men were hyped on adrenaline.

Brooke kicked her way through the shattered remains of the meal on the floor. "Stop it, Jordan. *Now.*"

Somehow her calmly spoken words in conjunction with the reverberation of her stamped high heel must have penetrated his rage. He turned to look at her.

Thank God Adam quickly grabbed and pinned both of Parker's wrists behind his back before her oldest brother could make a furtive move to take advantage of Jordan's distraction.

Anna rushed past a toppled chair to stand beside Brooke, sliding an arm around her shoulders. "Parker, put a lid on it. You're upsetting your sister and that can't be good for her in her condition." She rested a hand on her own slight baby bump. "Or my condition, either, for that matter. Can't you see Brooke's swaying on her feet?"

Brooke winced. She hated sounding like a wimp, but it did seem to take the wind out of the sails for both men. Parker eyed Jordan warily while Jordan strode back to her side.

"Do you feel all right?"

Not really, but the last thing she wanted was to launch another argument of people blaming each other for upsetting the pregnant women.

Brooke chose her words carefully. "I'm upset. Who wouldn't be? I didn't expect that everyone would do a happy dance, but I expected civility."

Anna stared down her husband.

Parker grimaced. "Damn. Sorry, Brooke. The last thing I want is to do anything that would harm you or your baby. You're my sister, kid, I just…" He shook his head as if to clear away the fog of rage. "I just didn't think."

She noticed he hadn't apologized to Jordan, but she figured it was best to leave that one alone for now. At least they weren't hitting each other anymore.

"Lissette," Anna, the ever-efficient, called, taking charge, "the dinner table is out of commission for tonight. So I believe we'll all have a light supper out on the veranda. It's a lovely temperate evening. Have the cook bring us something simple, whatever she can put together quickly."

Brooke could hear the implied part of quick, meaning they wouldn't have to endure this horrible gathering much longer.

Anna hooked her arm through Brooke's and ushered her toward the door. "Let's find a lounger where you can put those feet up."

"That obvious they're swollen, huh?"

Bonita joined alongside them with an unsteady gait. "You should quit trying to squeeze your feet into those heels. When I was carrying you and Brittany, my ankles swelled up like balloons. You girls caused me trouble from the first trimester and haven't stopped since." She tossed back the last of her drink, extending it for someone to refill.

Brooke wondered if she could borrow some armor to wear around her mother. Or earplugs. How come everyone else seemed able to ignore the comments except her?

Luckily, Lissette was otherwise occupied which sent a frowning Bonita off hunting for her own damn refill. Hopefully, the decanters would be empty.

Brooke swung wide the double doors to the veranda. A gust of fresh night air caressed over her with a much-needed cleansing freshness. She turned to speak to Jordan—only to find he'd stayed behind with Parker.

They weren't throwing punches, but their intense expressions showed their words were equally as powerful. Just her luck, the high ceilings bounced echoes around like racquetballs. Every word of their exchange pummeled her.

Parker stuffed his hands in his pockets. "I always knew you were ruthless, but I never suspected you would sink so low as to deliberately knock up my sister to secure a piece of the Garrison pie."

She heard Jordan deny it. Heard him tell Parker what an ass he was and how Emilio already owned a piece of Garrison Incorporated. Besides, Jefferies Enterprises could take on Garrison just fine on its own.

Brooke heard it all. Yet still, after a lifetime

of growing up in a family that didn't know the meaning of enough power, she couldn't help but wonder if Parker was right.

Four

Standing behind Brooke outside her condo door after the family dinner from hell, Jordan worked his jaw side to side. Parker Garrison packed a mean right hook. Not that Jordan planned on admitting it.

At least he'd given as good as he'd taken. And he had to confess, after so many years of contention between them, it had felt damn great to let loose on the guy.

Except then he'd looked up and seen Brooke's pale face.

Jordan hadn't realized until then how emotional the cool beauty could be. The family's disapproval really had her worried. He would have taken them all on if he hadn't seen how fast they backed off once they, too, noticed how the confrontation upset her.

Well, everyone except their sloshed mother.

He hadn't been predicting a red carpet reception, but he'd expected basic courtesy, more like what they'd settled into afterward during the cool—brief—dinner on the veranda.

Jordan reached to touch Brooke's shoulder just as she opened the door and stepped into her condo. Closing the door behind him, he sealed them both in the sleek silver and pink luxury of her home. What a strange time to realize that while he'd viewed every inch of her luscious naked body, he'd never seen where she lived. Now he realized she had been keeping a part of herself from him by insisting they always meet at his place.

He took in the luxury living space sprawling in front of him in a study of silver, white and pinks. Definitely a woman's domain. No question, it was stylish and high-end, but not a place where he could see himself relaxing. He had a quick mental flash of his own childhood home, as swank as the Garrison complex...

But a hell of a lot warmer.

Jordan brushed aside thoughts that didn't change a thing about his path with this woman. If he let Brooke see the slightest chink in his resolve, they would be toast. Even now, he could tell from the brace of her shoulders and the way she chucked her purse onto the sofa, tension still lingered.

He closed the distance between them and rested his hands on her shoulders. He responded to the feel of her beneath his hands. His body aroused in mere seconds any time he got near her these days. But, yeah, she was definitely tense.

Jordan rubbed his thumbs along the kinked muscles in her neck, considering all the ways a man could help a woman relieve this kind of stress. The possibilities tantalized. "Are you going to tell me what's going on with the silent treatment, or do I have to start playing twenty questions?"

He leaned to kiss the nape of her neck, taking his time to absorb the scent of her. She swayed toward him with a whisper of a moan. Then he could almost feel the return of her resolve starch up her straightening spine.

She shrugged off his hands and turned on her heel, her Garrison chin firmly set for battle. "Is it true what my brother said back at the house, right after your fight? Did you sleep with me just to gain a deeper toehold in the Garrison empire? Did you try to get me pregnant on purpose?"

Crap. She'd overheard? Jordan clenched his jaw, then winced at the stab of pain. He hoped Parker was enjoying at least a couple of bruised ribs.

"Ah, the whole Garrison-Jefferies rivalry." He considered the best way to reassure her. She likely wouldn't believe an outright denial anyway. And to be truthful, in the past, he'd done anything possible to get the inside track on Garrison, Incorporated.

Anything to get ahead. "It's a reality we both have to deal with. Isn't that why *you* slept with *me?* To piss off your family? What better way to strike back at big brother Parker and your mother."

"How can you think that?" Her brown eyes went wide, then definitely glinted with guilt.

He reminded himself of her pale face and kept his own stirring anger in check. "For the very same reason you believe the only reason I'm with you is to gain access to your family's stock."

Sure, a union between them made good business sense. But he also couldn't miss that the more time he spent with Brooke, the less he thought about corporations. The apartment dates, with just the two of them, had given him far more insight about her than twice as many outings in a distracting public crowd could have.

Pointedly, he held her gaze until finally she looked down and away, striding toward the kitchen in an obvious move to avoid him. "We don't have much reason to trust each other, do we?"

He watched her walk, the gentle sway of her hips beneath the dark clingy fabric, the hint of bare calf at the slit of her hem. His mind mentally traveled up that patch of skin to silky thigh.

"I guess not." Following her, he lounged in the archway linking the kitchen to the dining area, trying to hang on to the conversation long enough to address her fears about him. "How do we get past that?"

"More dating?" She pulled out a large bottled water from the refrigerator and filled two crystal glasses. "Time."

"Exactly." He'd solidified his point about dating. Apparently he'd done well enough in hiding his own restlessness. And since he didn't want to let on that his thoughts kept straying to her possible choice of lingerie tonight, he distracted himself with figuring out what it was about this place and her mother's home that bugged him.

He took the glasses from her, returned to the living room and set their drinks on the coffee table. "How about we start small tonight?"

"What do you mean?" She eyed him suspiciously.

"Let's sit." He would make her more comfortable by connecting with her the best way he knew how. Their words might do battle, but the heat between them had always been in perfect harmony.

Warily, she perched on the edge of the over-stuffed white sofa. "Okay? What now?"

"Do you trust me with your feet?"

"That's a strange question."

Kneeling in front of her, he pulled off her shoes and tossed the high heels under the coffee table. He sat on the sofa and swung her legs onto his lap, gripping her feet in his hands. He kept his eyes off the way her hem hitched higher, knowing he'd never survive this if he continued torturing himself with thoughts of undressing her. Instead, his thumbs worked a gentle massage along the arch of her instep.

"Ahhh…" Her head slumped sideways to rest against the couch. "Uhmmm, okay…"

The sweet hum of approval in her throat would have encouraged any man, and he looked forward to hearing her make that same sound when he touched her in many, many more places. "I take that as consent to continue."

"A definite yes." She reached behind her and cleared away half of the pink throw pillows so she could settle into the crook of the sofa.

Her shoulder shifted, sending her full breasts in a tantalizing shimmy of movement while she made herself more comfortable. His mouth went dry, and he reached for his water. He'd been with too many women to count, and none had this powerful effect on him.

After he replaced his half-empty water glass on the coffee table, he pressed his thumbs back into the graceful arch of her right foot and decided to see if he could tease a smile back to her face. "Since you're in a yes mood, how about you marry me?"

She didn't so much as flinch, much less open her eyes. "Don't push your luck."

"Can't blame a guy for trying."

Sure enough, the corners of her mouth twitched with a grin as she relaxed deeper into the cushions, hugging one of those froufrou pink pillows.

The business world hadn't labeled him persistent without cause. He would win her over. He was patient as well as persistent, a combination for success.

Never had the stakes been so high, and not just on the business front. He refused to let his child be born without his name. From a young age, he'd known too well how vulnerable a young kid could be without a father.

He'd been told how Emilio's biological father had abandoned his responsibilities. When Emilio's mother had died, Emilio would have become a ward of the state if Jordan's parents hadn't adopted their nanny's orphaned son.

Jordan refused to be like the man who'd left an innocent kid alone and helpless. Sure Brooke had plenty of family, but never would he let his child wonder why his own father hadn't cared enough to be there.

His hands gripped tighter around Brooke's feet as if he could somehow will her to stay with him. "You're just as sexy in sandals as you are in heels."

She opened one eye to peek at him. "Are you jumping on my mother's bandwagon and telling me I have fat feet?"

He would rather guide conversations away from that drunken bat. "You have beautiful feet, with pretty red toenails. I just want to know why you won't pamper yourself. Take it easy during your pregnancy."

"I'm letting you pamper me right now. Don't ruin it by grouching at me." The hint of a pout on her lips gave him an almost irresistible urge to mold her mouth against his for a taste.

"Fair enough." He let his hands glide up to her ankles, his touch growing lighter.

When she didn't object, he inched his way higher to her calves, more of a stroke now than a massage against her bare flesh. Her honey-toned skin still carried a light tan left over from the summer.

Her chest rose and fell evenly. Had she fallen asleep? He skimmed his fingers to the back of her knees, a place he remembered well as being an erogenous zone. Her breathing hitched, then increased.

Oh, yeah. Her eyes might be closed but she was totally awake and not stopping him.

He could continue farther up her dress, likely without protest from her. But he'd better not take the risk now. He'd won time with her. He needed to use it wisely.

Jordan inched his hands from beneath the hem of her dress.

Her lashes fluttered open, and her arms lifted.

Hell, yeah. He couldn't stop the smile from sneaking over his face, and she grinned back. So he waited for her to make the next move.

Her arms hooked around his neck as her mouth parted to greet his with a sigh of acceptance. He wanted to touch all of her, but restraint seemed to be working more in his favor. He planted his hands on either side of her on the couch, careful to keep his full weight off her. As much as he ached for closer contact, he needed to be careful of the growing swell of her stomach. Why couldn't she see that he simply wanted to take care of her and the baby?

He let the kiss play out, glad to connect with her on a level where they communicated so well. Angling to rest his weight on one elbow, he allowed his other hand free rein to roam along her side, upward to cup the fullness that had been tempting him all evening long. The near-immediate beading of her nipple through the fabric followed by that sweet hum of pleasure he'd been hoping to hear encouraged him.

Her slight wriggle against his thigh urged him to keep right on pursuing this path. But the more logical strategist in him knew better.

Damn.

Reason insisted if he took the easy way out for the sex he wanted so badly, he might never understand her reasons for resisting an engagement. Without that information, he would ultimately lose. He had one window of time to finalize this deal, and no amount of killer kisses or soft sighs of approval could sway him from closing the most important transaction of his life.

Jordan eased back with a final sweep of his tongue, a last nip on her bottom lip. "Not that I'm complaining, but what's going on here? I was expecting to work my ass off for a simple quick kiss."

She traced a fingernail along the back of his neck. "You said my swollen feet are pretty."

Women were more complicated than any boardroom negotiation he'd ever undergone. "Your feet are perfect, and if they're swollen, it's half my fault since it takes two to make a baby."

She'd mentioned the comment her mother made. Could a drunk mother's ridiculous throwaway comment bother such a successful, confident woman?

Of course it could. And what a strange time to notice there were no photos of her parents in the condo that he could see. In fact, the walls and mantle bore just watercolor artwork. The only photo he could find…a small photo in a silver frame on the end table. He scooped it up to find five young Garrisons on the beach, Brooke and Brittany not more than five or six. His thumb gravitated to the image of Brooke, no questioning which was her with that sneaky strand of hair sliding from her ponytail.

Brooke raked her fingernail from the back of his neck around to trail along his sore jaw. "I'm sorry my brother hit you."

"I'm not." He smiled in spite of himself and replaced the photo on the end table. "That was the most fun I've had in a long time."

"You're crazy."

"It's a man thing. I expected it." He shrugged off the fight and stifled a wince at his wrenched shoulder as he sat up again. He tugged Brooke to sit in the crook of his arm. "Since we've told the family, what do you say tomorrow we go out to dinner on our own? I'll pick you up after work."

"Why don't we meet here at my place instead?"

She plucked at the hem of her loose-fitting black dress. "Or we can meet at yours and dine on the balcony again."

He frowned. "You don't want to go out with me."

"It's not that." She kept picking at the fabric, her fingers pinching a loose thread with unwavering attention. "I'm just not ready for things to be so...public."

Jordan walled off his impatience. He was starting to learn that while this Garrison had a reputation for being less confrontational than the rest, she was still every bit as stubborn in her own way. "What sort of timetable do you have for telling the rest of the world this is my baby?"

"I'll know when it's right." She finally snapped the stray thread on her dress and pulled a tight smile.

He could already see how much the thought of making this decision was torturing her. Informing her family had taken her months. Taking him to dinner had left her pale, her hands clammy and her feet puffy.

How much more stress would it bring her figuring out how to tell her workmates and the rest of South Beach about their relationship? Without a doubt, gossip would flow. Things had only begun to die down from Emilio and Brittany hooking up. And while Emilio as a partner in Jefferies Brothers had his own issues with Garrison, Incorporated, the animosity between Jordan and Parker went off the charts.

Brooke had to know the baby's paternity would be grist for a hungry rumor mill.

He studied the dark circles under her eyes and made an executive decision. The sooner everyone knew about their romance, the better. And by everyone, he meant all of South Beach in one fell swoop.

Jordan tipped a knuckle under Brooke's chin and brushed a final kiss across her lips. "All right, then, as you said, when the time is right, the world will know."

The next morning, Brooke raced past her personal assistant at the condominium development with a smile and a wave, late, thanks to her restless dreams about Jordan. The massage had tweaked her every last hot button, convincing her that having Jordan in her bed again would be a very delicious idea. But he'd pulled back when she'd been wanting, forcing her to think about their future and not just her keen hunger for him.

Her waking thoughts were equally as agitating as she recalled his kiss…and the way his thumb had gone straight to her image in the photo. He'd known the difference between her and her twin even as children. God, that rocked her.

She only half registered her assistant's call of, "You have a visitor," before Brooke threw wide the door to her office to find—

Her mirror image.

Well, her mirror image without a baby bulge since her twin wasn't five months pregnant. "Good morning, Britt. If you wanted the scoop about Jordan, we could have done lunch today and talked about your wedding plans at the same time."

In spite of being twins, they hadn't always been as close as Brooke would have wished. Brittany had often complained that everyone treated her like a child. However, since Brittany's engagement to Emilio, she'd become closer to her family.

Brittany leaned forward, gripping the portfolio briefcase on her lap tightly. "Are you all right?"

Brooke sank into a chair across from her sister rather than sitting behind the desk. "Yesterday's showdown with the family wasn't fun by any means, but at least that hurdle is passed. Mother reacted pretty much as expected, and both men walked away without broken bones."

"And?"

"And what?"

Brittany eased back in her chair, her eyes sympathetic. "You didn't read local newspapers over breakfast this morning."

The papers? A bad feeling shivered up her spine. "I overslept. I grabbed a bagel on my way out the door." A bagel the baby suddenly seemed determined to kick repeatedly. "Why?"

Her twin opened the monogrammed portfolio bag and pulled out a newspaper—the *South Beach Journal*.

Brittany flipped the paper open. "You're the lead

feature in the social section. Or rather, I should say, that you and Jordan are big news."

Brooke's stomach settled with a dull thud, followed by a roaring denial in her head. Blinking fast, she wiggled her fingers for the paper and sure enough, the lead story plastered a photo of her beside a photo of Jordan.

The paper shook in her hand. "How many more?"

"Three that I've seen, and, of course, it's on the Internet." Brittany twisted her princess-cut yellow diamond engagement ring around and around her finger. "I hear big cash offers are already starting to roll in for the first photo of the two of you together."

"Great." Brooke slammed the paper closed. "That makes me feel much better."

"You could pose and donate the proceeds to charity."

"Don't make light of this, please. This is my life. My baby's life." She blinked back tears of frustration. "This explains why Parker has been trying to reach me all morning. I thought he wanted to badger me about Jordan, so I ignored the messages from his receptionist, Sheila, uh…" Brooke pressed her fingers to her aching temple, the woman's full name escaping her.

"McKay." Brittany finished her twin's sentence. "Sheila McKay."

"Yeah, right. Although learning the reason for the calls from his receptionist doesn't make me any more inclined to answer." She glanced down at the paper again. "I wonder if Jordan knows yet. Damn. What am I saying? Of course he knows. Mr. Perfect would never oversleep and miss checking the news."

"Emilio has already gone to see Jordan and make sure his head doesn't explode over this."

Brooke swiped away a lone tear. She hated feeling so out of control of her life, a by-product of growing up with an alcoholic mother, no doubt. She could only imagine how someone as strong-willed as Jordan would react to having his life scooped this way. "I wonder which of Mother's staff sold the story."

"It could be anyone. We have so many people in and out of there making deliveries with my wedding less than three weeks away."

"I'm sorry to add stress during what should be a happy time."

"Shush. It doesn't have to be all about me. As a matter of fact, it feels good to be able to offer support for a change instead of always being the one needing it."

"Thank you for being here. It's going to be tough winning over the brothers. And I don't even want to think about Mother." Brooke shuddered.

"Of course, I'm here. I owe you, anyway. Remember when the news rag got the pictures of me making out with the chauffeur and you told Mother and Dad it was you? Since you never got in trouble, they let you off with a slap on the wrist. Me, I would have lost my car."

Brooke welcomed the laughter to replace well-ing tears. "The shock on the chauffeur's face was priceless."

"No kidding. If he couldn't tell us apart, then he didn't deserve to have me."

"Damn straight." Brooke's mind skipped back five months to the night she and Jordan made the baby, when he'd most definitely known one twin from the other. Still… "Everything is just changing too fast for me."

Brittany squeezed Brooke's hand. "Once Emilio and I are married, they'll be that much closer to realizing they have to accept all the Jefferies into the Garrison family. Maybe there will even come a time when Garrison, Incorporated can merge with Jefferies Brothers."

"Perhaps." Brooke forced a tight smile although she really wanted to scream. Even her own sister saw this relationship in terms of a business negotiation.

Still, Brooke wasn't so certain things would be settled with her family that easily.

By the end of the week, Jordan wondered why he hadn't managed to settle this wedding issue yet. He tried to take comfort in the relationship being public now. A Friday night dinner at a back table in his brother's restaurant counted as progress.

She hadn't been happy about the newspaper articles, but as he'd hoped when he'd had his secretary leak the story, Brooke had quit worrying about secrecy. They'd begun dating openly in earnest.

He had to admit, he'd enjoyed the hell out of the past week although he should be focusing on the upcoming opening of his Hotel Victoria. He had a stack of work and telephone messages sitting by his computer right now—although at least he could ignore the five messages from his ex. Damn, she was persistent. When she'd called out of the blue yesterday, he'd told her he was seeing someone else now. If she wouldn't listen to words, distance seemed the best option. His secretary would have to tell her he wasn't available.

Jordan put his ex-lover out of his mind, into his past, and realized he didn't feel the least regret. He had his mind and intentions firmly set elsewhere, something others began noticing, as well. Emilio had even caught him watching the clock during a late-day board meeting.

Of course, he didn't bother masking his attraction to her. While romancing Brooke every night this week, he'd also worked to win her over by easing tension with her family.

An unhappy family made for an unhappy Brooke.

So he'd taken Brooke to Brittany's restaurant/ lounge for supper one night. To her brother Adam's club another. He'd made a point of being where her family congregated, and sure enough, the press hadn't gotten over their fascination with snapping photos yet. He couldn't blame them. Candlelight played well across her beautiful face—and wreaked havoc with his self-control.

Still, in spite of his best efforts, aside from Brittany, the reception from the Garrison clan stayed at subarctic temperatures. The disapproval was starting to chafe.

He wanted to enjoy this Friday night away from her family, *without* thinking about another Sunday dinner with the Garrisons. His jaw still hurt from the last gathering. Not that he would ever let that arrogant ass Parker know.

Maybe he and Brooke could skip the family dinner if he came up with a better plan for the weekend, a different tactic for winning Brooke over. He'd been thinking how important it was for his child to know he or she had a father who cared, a father who was there. How he wouldn't be like Emilio's old man and run out on responsibilities.

Perhaps Brooke needed a reminder of the scars an absentee father could leave on a child.

Jordan waited for the waitress to finish serving their after-dinner lattes before he reached across to take her hand. "Would you like to fly down to the Bahamas and get away from the paparazzi?"

Her eyes lit as bright as the oversized flickering candle between them. "Yes."

His hand over hers, he thumbed along the soft inside of her palm. "Visit your half sister."

"Definitely, yes." She sagged back in her seat, the relaxed atmosphere of the nightclub and music appearing to calm her more than anything else this week.

Might as well go for broke. He explored the smooth skin and perfect manicure. "And tie the knot."

She snatched her hand away. "No, thank you."

He kept his smile in place and chased her hand back down, soothing her with a kiss over her knuckles. He lingered to nip the gold band on her thumb. "Can't blame a guy for trying."

She narrowed her eyes. "I can stop dating a guy who won't listen."

That caught him off guard. He never overplayed his hand. Although it had been a while since he'd dated, after all. In fact, he'd broken things off with his last relationship shortly before that first night with Brooke.

And there hadn't been anyone since then. A fact he wasn't ready to consider for too long. "You would really cut us off from being together, after the great week we've had, just because I want to marry you?"

"I don't like being manipulated."

A smart man listened, and he'd never been accused of being stupid. "I asked you a simple question, which you answered. I'll back off."

"As long as you understand. I watched my parents live in a loveless marriage. It destroyed them and hurt all of us. Maybe that's something you can't grasp."

Apparently he hadn't overplayed at all. She'd just shared a vital piece of information with him. But Jordan also understood that he had pushed as far as he could for one night. He'd won on the dating issue, and that was going well. So he would continue with the dates. Have her sister Cassie add persuasive insights for Brooke. Let the romantic Bahamas work some magic.

And keep the engagement ring/wedding band set in his pocket ever-ready for use.

Five

The Bahamas midday sun baking overhead, Brooke stared out the limousine window and stretched her legs in front of her. The hem of her skirt teased her calves, her whole body hyperaware of the smallest caress ever since Jordan had reawakened every last hungry hormone inside her. Who would have thought a pregnant women could be so sensually focused on a nonstop basis?

Brooke plucked at her loose peasant blouse, the limo suddenly stuffy. Their morning flight had been early and a bit tiring, but already she could feel the tension seeping from her muscles with each mile closer to seeing her half sister. And how awesome to be away from all the media scrutiny.

If only her need for Jordan didn't make her so physically edgy.

She couldn't deny that Jordan had come up with the perfect way to spend their weekend. She only wished she could gauge *his* feelings. The man never gave anything away. He just kept that sexy smile and sleepy-eyed look focused on her, always lightly, teasingly touching her in some way.

Like now.

Jordan's thumb caressed the inside of her wrist. "How do you feel?"

Oh, if only he knew. She'd entertained the most vivid dreams about him just the night before, her imagination cut loose in sleep to imagine all the things he could do to her body with just his talented touch.

"I'm fine, just a little tired. But mellow, totally." She swept a hand to encompass the seaside road leading up to her sister's estate in an exclusive gated community of stucco homes. "Who wouldn't be relaxed at a place like this?"

"You should take it easy," he said for about the fiftieth time this week, making her wonder if he was avoiding her bed out of concern for her health.

"It's not as if I worked this morning. I only flew in an airplane, for goodness' sake. I even called my doctor before we left to get an official okay to travel. Remember?"

"I want to meet this guy." A twitch flicked in the corner of his eye. "Check his credentials."

She resisted the urge to go on the defensive. Of

course he wanted to interview the physician who would deliver their child. She would feel the same way in his position.

"*Her* credentials, and you can come to the next appointment."

"That's it?" His tic stopped. "No arguing?"

"My family always says I'm the peacemaker type."

"Peacemaker." He frowned. "I would rather you be honest with me than hide your feelings."

That sounded too much like the start of a conversation that could steal her deliciously pleasant imaginings of running her hands down his bare, sun-warmed chest. Thank goodness the limo pulled to a stop outside her sister Cassie's rambling home. She'd seen Cassie often enough since their father's will was read, but this was the first time Brooke had visited the Bahamas mansion.

The driver opened her car door, and she swung her legs out. Conversation would have to wait anyway as her sister already waited for her on the front porch, a towering man just behind her—Brandon Washington, Cassie's fiancé and the Garrison family lawyer.

Gold-and-green garland framed the entranceway and the couple, reminding Brooke that holidays should be spent with relatives. Cassie had lost not only her father this year, but her mother, as well. Brooke was glad to see that Cassie appeared to be moving past the grief and on with her life.

If only they could have consoled each other.

However, forging a relationship with Cassie had taken all the Garrison siblings time. Brooke resolved to lure Brittany here with her once things settled down after the wedding.

Jordan's shadow stretched over her. Was the man able to sense when she even *thought* the word wedding?

The realization reminded her how dangerous it might be to indulge her fantasies about Jordan this weekend. She needed to be careful not to wade in over her head with this man, something she feared would be all too easy to do given the magnetic spell he held over her.

Brooke angled her head back to whisper, "Jordan, do you want to know what would honestly relax me the most right now?"

"Absolutely."

"Could you and Brandon make yourselves scarce so I can have some low-key alone time with my sister?"

Jordan squeezed her shoulder, tormenting her with all the things they shouldn't do this weekend. "Consider it done."

Brooke advanced the rest of the way up the stone stairs, a smile firmly in place, and blessedly she saw nothing but welcome in Cassie's outstretched arms. She stepped into the hug she had needed so desperately since telling her family about the baby.

Beside her, she could see the men shaking hands

and thumping each other on the back as Brandon extended his congratulations.

Brooke's eyes filled with tears, and Cassie pulled back, tut-tutting. "No, no, this is a happy time. Dry up those tears."

"Hormones. I can't help it." She swiped the back of her hand along her cheeks. "I'm sad, I cry. I'm happy, I cry."

"Fair enough, then. Let me look at you while you finish sopping up those tears." Her sister stepped back, smiling. "Pregnancy most definitely suits you. You're gorgeous."

Brandon whistled low. "Amen to that."

Cassie swatted him lightly on the stomach. "You could be a little less enthusiastic in saying that, my dear."

The high-powered attorney slung an arm around Cassie's shoulders and dropped an unabashedly adoring kiss on his fiancée's cheek. "I'm a one-woman man, and you know it."

Cassie softened against him, her marquise-cut diamond engagement ring glinting in the early-afternoon sun. "Just so you don't forget it."

Rings, rings everywhere. Brooke resisted the urge to stomp her foot in frustration.

It was as if Jordan had special ordered all these engaged couples and their happiness just to tempt her. Instead she felt tormented by the ease in the relationships of her siblings with their loved ones. This was how things should be.

She was right to stick to her guns about dating rather than jumping into some marriage of convenience.

Jordan clapped Brandon on the shoulder. "How about you give me a tour of the place while our ladies here talk baby stuff?"

"Sounds like a plan to me, Jefferies. Let's start out by the pool house bar." Their voices drifted on the sea breeze, leaving the sisters alone.

Brooke reached to hook arms with Cassie, relaxing when her sister seemed to have no problems with the continued affection. "Thank you for welcoming us on such short notice."

"It's no trouble at all."

"Are you sure? Our visit is so last minute. We can stay at the hotel."

Since the reading of their father's will, her sister controlled the Garrison Grand-Bahamas nearby.

"Don't be silly. I have plenty of room and kept Mother's staff after she passed. We're fine."

"Okay, then." Brooke walked alongside her over the threshold into the splendor of Cassie's home, a busy, wonderful mix of contemporary, colonial and Queen Anne. "I must admit I welcome the extra time with you. We have a lot of lost years to make up for."

"I always thought my life was full here, and my mother truly was okay without the trappings of a wedding ring or marriage certificate." Cassie's eyes lingered on a portrait of John Garrison with Cassie's mother, the bronzed beauty who had held his heart if not his name. "But now that the tension has passed since the reading of our father's will, I *am* enjoying having siblings. Of course the big family is nothing new to you."

Brooke tore her gaze away from the image of her father and continued with her sister toward glass doors leading outside to a dense garden. "Just because I grew up with brothers and a sister doesn't mean I value you any less. It just took me a while to see past…"

"My getting such a large portion of your family's estate?" Cassie sat on a stone bench near a huge fountain.

Brooke sagged to sit beside her, the verdant scents from the tropical flowers not strong enough to override the acrid air of betrayal. "Dad lying. You had the truth all those years. We had a lie. That was—still is—hard for me to see past." She slid her hands protectively over her stomach. "I want my child to have a life filled with the truth."

"So you came here for more than a place to prop your feet and sun your face."

Her mind crowded with images—that portrait of her father with his other family, so many engagement rings, and largest of all, Jordan's face coming toward hers for a mind-numbing kiss. "I think perhaps I came here for answers."

"Ah, sister dear, the problem is, just because I found a way or your other siblings did for whatever reason, doesn't mean that's right for you. Everyone has to find their own path."

Which left her with nothing more than a host of questions and two swollen feet. If only life were as simple as tossing a penny into that sparkling fountain so she could wish her world right again. She stared into the bubbling waters, her mind mixing around the images of the portrait, rings—Jordan's handsome face. Simply the thought of his kiss made her skin tingle all over as if she'd plunged herself into the fountain.

At this rate, how would she ever manage to resist falling into bed with him?

Moonlight glistening on the surf, Jordan looped his arm around Brooke's side and enjoyed the gentle kick of his child against his fingertips. The little one seemed restless tonight.

And something was up with the baby's mother, as well. He wasn't sure what churned around in that beautiful head of hers, but she'd been jittery since they'd arrived. Not the reaction he'd planned for.

He'd hoped bringing her here would advance his cause. With luck, this midnight walk by the water would calm her and romance her. But he wanted more than romance from her. He wanted commitment. He wanted to plant his ring on her finger the way Cassie Sinclair's hand sported Brandon's rock.

No question, Brandon was one astute dude on a lot of points. Brooke Garrison was a hot pregnant woman.

Her pink dress with the gauzy wrap draped around her shoulders complimented her new curves. The simple elegance seemed all the more perfect with her bare feet furrowing in the sand. He couldn't help but notice how her dress tied at the shoulders, simple little strings he could so easily tug and undo…

Stop. Many more thoughts like that and he would have her ducking behind a dune.

"How was your time with Cassie?" He thought of all those photos packed in every corner of the house. The outward structure of the place might resemble the South Beach Garrison mansion, but no question, John Garrison had found a home here. It was that element that had been missing from Bonita's house, even Brooke's condo. He just hadn't been able to pinpoint it until now. Could Brooke distinguish the difference?

"Good. Very good, actually. It's a journey forming a sister bond once we're already grown-ups, but we're definitely well on our way to the friends part." She kicked her way through the surf. "Cassie's an amazing person."

"All the Garrisons are definitely overachievers." He leaned in to sniff her neck, catch a hint of her perfume.

"Is that a compliment?" She tipped her head toward him, then pulled back as if reminding herself she shouldn't give in.

What might things be like between them once they got past all the stop-and-start negotiations of this marriage deal? A no-holds-barred Brooke was something he wanted to see.

"In my book it is." Their child would probably be a supercharged handful, and yeah, he looked forward to the challenge.

"Do you ever take vacations? Just pick up and leave all the work behind?"

"I'm here, aren't I?"

"You're here because you want to win me over. That's different."

She'd figured that out? He should have realized she would. Still, that didn't make the effort wasted, especially if it worked. "I'm lucky my job takes me to amazing places. I tag on an extra day to sightsee when I can."

"What about after the baby comes?"

Ah, now he saw where she was going with this, and he liked that her thoughts were finally on the future. "Obviously a child means we'll both make changes in our lifestyles. I expect that. I look forward to it."

Did she trust his answer? He couldn't tell, and she'd stopped talking so he searched for something to fill the silence that would reassure her. "I did just pick up and leave once, six months after I graduated from college. Emilio and I backpacked across Europe."

He hadn't thought about that awesome month in… Hell, he couldn't remember when he'd dredged up memories of that time.

She snuggled closer against his side as they strolled. "You're really close to your brother."

"We are. Always have been since we were kids. And now he's the only family I have left." Jordan paused. "Or rather, he was. Now I've got this baby—and you."

"Sounds like the perfect sort of vacation."

"It was great, until…" Crap. He'd meant to dig up pleasant words to soothe her.

"Until what?" She glanced up at him.

He settled for, "We went home."

"Come on, Jordan." She squeezed his side. "You've heard about me and my father and how painful the past months have been. This sharing thing needs to be a two-way street."

The pain of that time kicked over him. The power, even after so many years, surprised him more than a rogue wave. "We came home early because our parents died."

She stopped in her tracks, her hands falling to rest on his chest. "Oh, God, Jordan, I'm sorry. I knew they were dead, but I didn't realize you'd lost them both at the same time. That must have been so difficult for you. How did you lose them?"

"In a boating accident. Emilio and I came home from Europe and assumed control of the business in Dad's place."

"And you never took a vacation again." Her eyes glinted with a sympathetic air that made him uncomfortable.

He wanted to win her over, but not this way. "Like I said, I'm seeing the world on my terms.

When the baby comes, I get to make my own schedule because I'm the boss. I promise, the kid will get trips to Disney. Don't worry."

She stared into his eyes and he wondered if she would press him on the issue of his parents. He braced himself.

Finally, she looked away and started walking again. "So when this baby asks about how Mom and Dad met and decided to start a family, what do we say?"

Relieved to be off the hook from more emotional topics, he answered with the first thought that popped to mind. "We tell him or her the truth."

"The truth?" She snorted on a giggle. "Isn't that a bit much for a child?"

"Not the way I see it." His emotions still too damn raw, he needed—welcomed—the distraction of splaying his hands over her shoulders, sliding them up into her hair. A whiff of her perfume caught on the breeze to tempt him again.

"How do you see it?" Her words hitched with a betraying breathiness.

He stepped closer, skimming against her, each brush a hot temptation. "I would say that I saw a one-of-a-kind woman who knocked me off my feet."

Her chest swelled with a gasp, her fuller breasts pressing against him as she leaned. "That's nice."

"Not nice so much as smart. I know special when I see it." When he felt it. Like now. He soaked in the silkiness of her hair against his fingers.

Her lashes fluttered closed, then half-open again. "You're using those stellar corporate boardroom skills on me."

"Why is it so difficult for you to trust what I say?" He shoved aside a punch of guilt over the newspaper leak. He had been thinking of her peace of mind.

"It's been a tough few months, learning about my father." She waved a hand in the general direction of Cassie's house. "Finding out about this other life of his. It can shake a person's trust, especially when I already had doubts about the whole happily-ever-after gig in the first place."

"I can understand that." That wasn't what he'd intended in bringing her here, damn it. He worked to steer the conversation back on path. "My parents had a great marriage. I've seen how it should work."

"They loved each other?"

"Yes." The loss squeezed his gut again.

She stared at him. Waiting. For?

Hell. She was talking about that *L* word, or the lack thereof between them.

He'd promised to be honest with her. He'd been able to go to the press to make things easier for her, but this would be different. He knew that.

He hooked his hands behind her waist, wishing this could be simpler, wishing they were free to take their time and let the simmering passions and feelings build.

Then again, would they have ever made time for that to happen if not for the pregnancy? The sand shifted under him as he thought of all he would have missed if he'd stayed away from Brooke Garrison. "Feelings grow over time. We have a lot to build on."

"Thank you for being honest."

At least he'd answered right. An exhale of relief gushed out of him in time with the receding wave. The next curl of the ocean around their feet sent desire pumping through him, an urge to forge ahead. "Then let's be honest about what feelings we already have."

Feelings?

She was awash in them at the moment. Sensual longing more than tingled over her now. It burned until she ached to sink deeper in the waves for relief.

Or submerge herself in the sweet release she knew she could find in Jordan's arms.

Maybe that was her answer after all. Quit worrying so much about the rings and happily-ever-after family portraits. The baby wouldn't be born for a few more months. Why deny herself the pleasure of exploring what she and Jordan did have figured out? How to bring each other unsurpassed pleasure.

Before she could change her mind, Brooke tucked her hand behind his neck and arched up on her toes to press her mouth to his. His low growl of appreciation rumbled against her already sensitive breasts a second before his arms secured her to him.

Water soothed around her feet, languished warm liquid touches up her ankles as Jordan toyed with the knots holding her whole dress together. Silk swayed along her calves, teasing between her legs while his mouth covered hers, his kiss growing deeper, more insistent. Her fingers gripped his hair, holding him to her while she let the desire for him wash over her as relentlessly as the waves stole the sand from beneath her bare feet.

He palmed her bottom and nestled her closer, closer still, as near as she could get in her condition—and likely as far as they should take this out on an open beach.

She'd been wanting this, thinking of this. Why was she hesitating? She wouldn't. "Let's go to my room."

Six

At the bold scoop of Jordan's arm behind her knees, Brooke gasped with surprise. He gathered her up into his embrace and charged across the beach toward the private entrance to their suite. She laced her fingers behind his neck and held on, savoring the strength of his body and the fluid movement of muscle.

Her heart raced as fast as his feet. "I can walk, you know."

His hold merely tightened, tucking her hip close to the hard heat of him. "I'm not wasting any time for you to change your mind."

She threw back her head and laughed, the stars overhead not even close to competing with the sparks of sensation showering through her. She rested her head against his shoulder. "Not a chance of that. I want this. I want you."

"I'm not going to argue with you." He thundered up the lanai steps, across the small patio and angled to open the outside door to her room. His jaw slanted closer and on impulse, she arched up to brush a kiss along the bit of bruise that remained from his fight with her brother.

She would always associate the sweet scent of the greenery on the porch, the crash of the island waves with this moment, her senses all on high alert. He carried her over the threshold and lowered her to her feet. She sank her sandy toes in the thick rug and stretched upward.

Her hungry mouth locked to his, her fingers yanking at his shirt. The cotton fabric bunched in her fists still held the heat of his body which made her yearn all the more for the real thing. She flung away his shirt and flattened her palms to the pulsating warmth of his chest. She ached to feel that strength over her, under her, all over her.

Jordan swept away her shawl, the crocheted lace slithering down her body to pool around her ankles. The heat of his hands on her uncovered shoulders sent a shiver of anticipation through her.

He tugged the tie on one shoulder, then the other, the satiny top easing down until the fabric hitched on her breasts. Leaving her covered. For now. But thanks to the dress's built-in bra, once the top fell free she would be fully exposed.

Her hands gripped and twitched along the back of his neck, his bristly hair teasing along the sensitive pads of her fingertips. He murmured words of encouragement in her ear.

Not that she needed any. But the whisper of his breath against her skin incited a fresh wave of want.

Jordan slid his fingers under the gauzy fabric, teasing inside to test the creamy texture of one breast. The dress inched lower. Her breathing snagged in her throat.

She couldn't think of a time she'd ached for anything as much as she longed for the feel of his palms on her breasts, heavy with need.

"Jordan…" Was that husky plea hers?

His steamy gaze darn near seared through satin. The ties from one shoulder still in his hands, he teased the tip along her collarbone, over the top of her breasts. He nudged the dress lower bit by bit, layering kisses beneath each new patch of skin he unveiled. Finally, her satiny dress fell free from her chest, skimming down her body, leaving her wearing only panties, just a thin scrap of Lycra separating her from him. She pressed into his cupping palms with a needy groan as her dress joined her shawl around her ankles.

A moment's unease snaked through her as she wondered what he would think of the unmistakable differences in her body. She waited, her hands stilled on his chest by anticipation mixed with anxiety.

The night breeze through the open veranda doors did little to cool her overheated flesh. Jordan's hungry and oh so appreciative gaze upped her temperature even more. Her heart kicked into a speed that almost made her dizzy.

"And I thought you were beautiful before." His hands skimmed from her breasts to shape over her stomach.

He seemed to mean it and she exhaled her relief.

The baby booted him. He jerked a hand back, his eyes wide. "Wow, that was so…incredible."

She laughed, enjoying sharing this moment with him, having him touch their growing child. "Pretty intense, isn't it? It doesn't hurt, although this soccer star wakes me up sometimes."

He stared at her stomach, stunned as he placed his hand back again in a broad span of warmth. "Amazing." Eventually he looked back at her face again. "Are you sure we're clear to take this further?"

Unease—and she hated to admit it, even a touch of insecurity—crept back up her spine. "Are you going to be one of those men who's afraid to touch a pregnant woman?"

"Hell, no," he answered without hesitation. "But I also think I should be man enough to check about restrictions."

"No restrictions. Well, except we can't pull out a trapeze."

"You would have used a trapeze before?"

She rolled her eyes, but welcomed how his charm eased some of the starch from her spine. "In your dreams."

Brooke relaxed against him, the brush of her legs against his dragging her back under his spell.

His hands roved over her with unmistakable impatience. "I'm not much for circus tights, anyhow. So other than the trapeze?"

"Pretty much anything goes as long as it's comfortable." Although she did remember one chapter in her *What to Expect* book that had interesting possibilities. "As the baby grows, I will need to use inventive positions."

"Inventive positions with me, you mean."

"Possessive, aren't you?"

He stayed silent, his face solemn for three slow blinking seconds before he smiled deep creases into his face. "Let's get back to those inventive positions."

"I'm not that large yet."

"We could always practice now."

Practice for later? Assuming they would still be together and having sex when her pregnancy advanced to that stage months from now. The intimate, vulnerable image sent a shiver through her.

"You're sexy now," he whispered against her ear and nipped her diamond stud between his teeth. "You'll be even more so then because it's my baby you're carrying."

"You're a smooth talker." She backed him toward the bed, brushing against the unmistakable reaction to her nakedness.

"I mean what I say." He closed his eyes briefly as she continued to skim against him, his throat moving in a long, slow swallow. "It doesn't pay to be caught in a lie."

"But you leave out parts of the truth."

"Then, I guess you will have to ask the right questions."

Just what she wanted to hear. She flattened her hand to his chest. "Do you want me to touch you here?"

"What do you think?" He stared down at her with eyes blue-flame hot.

"Answer, please." Yes, she wanted, needed the words.

"I've wanted your hands on me every damn second of every day since you left me in that hotel bed over five months ago."

He couldn't be much clearer than that. She wondered if there had been other women since then, but given his propensity for honesty, she wasn't sure she could handle the answer.

"Nobody but you since that night." His hands slid into her hair and tipped her face to his where she could see the honesty of his words.

She tried not to show how much that meant to her, tried not to *let* it mean so much to her. "Are you a mind reader, too?"

"Not a mind reader, but fairly good at judging expressions." His fingers traced down her spine. "A boardroom necessity."

"Remind me not to play cards with you." But back to the more pressing questions for the moment, something that seemed all the more urgent with his hands curved to her bottom. "Do you want my hand higher while I kiss you…or lower?"

"See if you can read my expression."

It seemed she had fairly astute expression-reading skills herself. Brooke arched up on her toes to press her lips to his while skimming her fingers down, down, down until they skimmed the heavy hard length of his arousal.

No question, he wanted her.

Her senses seemed more finely tuned than ever before, her awareness sharply honed. Any apprehensions she may have had about baring her pregnant body to his gaze evaporated under the obvious heat and passion of his attention.

His tongue dipped and swooped through her mouth while he made swift work of his shirt buttons and flung the garment away, quickly bringing them flush against each other. Flesh meeting flesh.

She sighed. The sweet abrasion of his bristly hair brought her breasts to tight peaks of near unbearable pleasure until she couldn't stop herself from wriggling against him. Wanting more. Already craving release.

"Patience, Brooke. Patience."

Damn it all. She was the most patient, calm person on the planet. If she wanted something now she deserved to have it.

Jordan trailed a finger down her spine until he

reached the top on her bikini panties resting just below the slight bulge of her stomach.

She stopped her caress and reached around to clamp his wrist. "I'm not getting fully naked until you lose more clothes."

He grinned. "What a hardship." Jordan spread his arms wide. "Have your way with me, woman."

Brooke unbuckled his belt and slid the leather free slowly, deliberately, then giving the length a shake and snap that echoed through the room.

Jordan's eyes widened. "My quiet one has even more fire than I knew."

Laughing, she tossed away his belt and grabbed hold of his pants. She tugged him forward and nipped his collarbone, while opening his zipper fly. "Still interested in talking?"

"Uh, not so much."

"Thought so." She slipped her hands into his pants and shoved them down and off in a deft sweep that left him gloriously naked. "Now don't move until I tell you."

Finally, finally she could touch him again and she let herself. Let her fingers, just the tips, glide over him along his chest, arms, wrists and hands.

His muscles rippled from the restraint of standing still when she could see clearly in his eyes that he wanted to leap forward. Tanned, defined abs begged for her attention and she obeyed, then surveying lower, lingering.

She remembered well the feel of wrapping her

legs around his solid thighs, then inching higher to dig in her heels. She adored the feel of those strong and powerful legs and worked her way back up again until her palms cupped his hips, and she stood face-to-face with him.

What new things would they try tonight?

She saw his biceps contract for action a split second before he scooped her up into his arms again. Brooke squeaked. "Stop! You really should stop carting me around this way. I'm too heavy."

"Not even close." He carried her past the settee over to the sprawling bed and gently settled her into the middle of the puffy comforter.

"My turn," he growled, and before she could answer—not that she could find words at the moment—his mouth closed over her breast.

Slowly, torturously so, he began his journey over her body, a trek that mirrored her exploration of his, except he kissed, licked, sipped his way over her heated skin and sensitive crooks until her fists twisted in the sheets. Until muttered pleas whispered on panting sighs.

Jordan grabbed a pillow and tucked it beneath her hips, offering the perfect angle to compensate for the gentle swell of her stomach. He slid over her, bracing his weight on his elbows and stared into her eyes, his heat pressing, waiting.

She flung her arms around his neck to urge him toward her for another of his mind-drugging kisses, but he wouldn't be budged. With slow deliberation, never looking away, refusing to let her so much as blink, he pressed inside her again, deeper. Fully. And waited.

If not for the stark strain of tendons budging on his neck, she wouldn't have known how dearly this restraint cost him. A fresh wave of pleasure scorched through her at his tenderness in the midst of such passion.

She arched up to kiss him, bit his lip and demanded, "More, now."

In case he might be left with any further doubts, she rolled her hips against his and, oh my, he got the message. Then she forgot about who was in control of the moment because it was all she could do to keep from screaming out her pleasure, which would only bring the whole house running. Instead, she buried her face in Jordan's shoulder and moaned a litany of encouragement to continue more of this, and yes, a little bit of that.

The rocking pressure of him moving in and out of her body brought back memories of their first time. The familiarity mixed with a sense of newness, risk, because they no longer had the option of walking away from each other forever.

A scary thought she shoved away before it could steal the blissful sensations tightening inside her. She grappled at his shoulders, scratched down his back then flattened her hands to absorb the warm feel of his sweat-slicked skin. Her fingers contracted again as the sweet need inside her rose higher, higher still until…

She dug her nails into his flesh, her head flinging back as she gasped once, again and again with the rippling waves of release. Dimly, she heard him join her as the tide seeped back out, leaving her limp and panting as he slumped over to lay beside her.

Their hitching breaths mingled in the light breeze swirling through the room. She rested her head on his chest and knew there was some reason she should gather her scrambled thoughts. Except that would require, well, the ability to think.

For some reason, her brain never worked as advertised when it came to dealing with Jordan.

Languid from loving and being loved, Brooke kept her arm over her eyes and felt the cool drift as Jordan slid the sheet from her, wafted it in the air and covered her body.

And left.

Watching from the veil of her eyelashes, she saw him tug on his boxer shorts before padding across the room to open the French doors. Her muscles pretty much mush after round two, she couldn't bring herself to slide from the bed, but that certainly wouldn't stop her from enjoying the view. Moonlight streamed over his golden nakedness, the broad planks of his steely shoulders.

He seemed so solid *and* exciting. Could she trust her judgment? Jordan had such sound arguments for why they should be together, and without a doubt what they'd shared in the bed had been beyond compare.

She'd thought she could be happy simply enjoying the sexual side of their relationship, but with the cool splash of air bringing a dose of reality, she couldn't ignore more rational thoughts nudging her as firmly as the tiny foot under her ribs.

Was she greedy to want more from Jordan? What she saw in Cassie and Brandon's eyes for each other?

Not that she begrudged her half sister her happiness. Heaven knew, Cassie deserved every bit of her hard-won peace after the tumultuous childhood she'd suffered as John Garrison's illegitimate child.

Brooke wrapped her arms around her own baby protectively and rolled from her side to her back.

Her parents' mixed-up union had caused so much pain for so many. John Garrison had hurt Cassie by never committing to her mother in much the same way Bonita and John had torn each other to shreds—yet never letting each other go.

Relationships were complicated enough in and of themselves. Add children and the issues multiplied exponentially.

Brooke turned back to stare at Jordan's toned body clad only in his boxers. He could take over her life as fully as his long-limbed body had sprawled over the bed after he finished loving her.

She needed to be more careful than ever to keep a close guard on her emotions.

Seven

Jordan usually hated those first few moments of waking when he had no guard over his thoughts.

This morning, however, he could find plenty to be happy about. Starting with the woman whose bottom snuggled against him, her warm bare skin and the rustle of sheets stirring memories of the night before.

Being with Brooke had been even more amazing than he'd remembered—and his recollections were mighty amazing. His plan for her to grow closer to him was working.

He hadn't, however, expected how much he would be drawn to *her*.

For about five seconds he tried to convince

himself it had to be because he'd been without since the night they'd shared in the Garrison Grand. Even when his ex-girlfriend had tried to lure him back into her bed, he hadn't been tempted. They'd been connected through business dealings, but that's all it could be. Memories of Brooke had tormented him then and now, ensuring his ex-lover held no more appeal.

Fresh flowers by the bed wafted sweet scents and an idea his way. He reached past her to snag an orchid from the vase. She'd told him once that she no longer suffered from morning sickness, so he figured it was safe to approach her.

Jordan sketched the flower along her jaw. "Are you awake?"

"Little bit." She inhaled with a low hum of appreciation.

Nuzzling her ear, he grazed the flower along her arm, teasing the inside of her elbow. "Wanna be more so?"

She mumbled something half-intelligible. He grazed the flower around her breasts until she peered over her shoulder at him with sultry sleepy eyes. He recalled well that same expression as he stared back at her on top of him when they'd explored more of the positions that best accommodated her pregnancy.

He grinned back at her. "I was thinking we could start working on another of those inventive positions."

She tried to roll to face him, but he kept her trapped in place with his legs.

"Don't I get to touch you?"

"We can touch very soon, beautiful, very soon." His throbbing body echoed the sentiment.

Jordan skimmed the flower lower, along her stomach, over her hip to the very top of her thigh. She wriggled with eagerness. At the glide of her hair against his chest, he almost dropped the orchid.

She snatched the flower from him. "Enough. More."

He couldn't help but smile at her contradictory words. Her intent, though, he understood. He slid his fingers between the juncture of her thighs, teasing the core of her and finding her ready for him. She arched against his fingers with that sweet whimper of hers that made him want more—more of her, more time to explore all of those positions. Even the less inventive ones as long as she was the woman under him.

She grabbed his wrist to halt his play, her fingernails stabbing into his skin and not distracting him in the least from what he wanted. "Jordan, either you finish or let me take over."

No misunderstanding that.

Jordan hooked a hand under her knee for just the right angle to slide inside her. Her damp heat clamped around him in time with his own groan. He buried his face in her silky hair, making the most of the advantageous position to stroke her breasts, so full and apparently sensitive if her writhing response offered any indication.

Their gentle rocking set the sheet slithering to the floor, the brush of chilly morning air doing little to cool the sweat beading on his body. The sunrise slanted through the blinds to play along the creamy expanse of her skin. He set his teeth to hold back the driving need to finish. He would wait for her, watch for signals of her nearing satisfaction.

And *yes,* his focused attention paid off. Her skin began to flush, her head arching back as she panted faster, faster still…

She gasped out a litany of need as she came apart, taking him along with her in a mind-blowing explosion of sensation. His forehead fell to her shoulder, his eyes closed while he simply *felt.* Her. All around him, against him. Aftershocks rocked through her so hard she shook in his arms, finally settling with a sated sigh.

As he stroked a hand through her hair, he thought again of how much he enjoyed how she made her needs heard in bed. If he could just get her to be as communicative about her thoughts. Because while she'd been physically responsive, he couldn't miss that this time she'd held something back. She'd shuttered her eyes from him at the last minute as if closing herself off from him.

He was losing ground at a time when he should be gaining. What the hell had gone wrong?

More importantly, he needed a plan to get back on track with planting his engagement ring on her finger.

* * *

Sunday night, Brooke forced her feet to climb the steps toward her mother's front door, Jordan only an inch from her side. She couldn't decide which was worse—facing her mother or going back through the gate past the snap-happy reporters intent on snagging photos.

She gripped Jordan's elbow tighter for support. As much as she'd been shaken by making love with him again and even feared how easily he could steal her willpower, she couldn't help wishing they'd been able to stay in the Bahamas a while longer. But she'd promised Brittany they would go over last-minute wedding plans tonight.

The decorated door loomed, bracketed by ornate porch lamps and twinkling garland.

"Hey, beautiful?" Pausing on the top step, he stroked her cheek, thumb grazing her lips with the tempting familiarity of lovers. "You look like you're heading to the gallows. We can always turn around and leave right now."

Mother or the media? Tough choice. But there were others to consider.

"We skipped the dinner part of the evening." She repressed a shudder at the thought of sitting for a meal with all that dissension stirring as tangibly as her roiling stomach. "The least we can do is show up for dessert since I promised Brittany. It's not like I can exactly hide from my family forever."

"You're not alone facing them anymore."

A sad smile tugged at her lips and heart. "A blessing and a curse."

He cocked an eyebrow. "Thanks."

Contrition nipped. She shouldn't take out her bad mood on him. "Sorry, I didn't mean that the way it—"

His thumb tapped her mouth closed. "You don't have to be the peacemaker with me. I'm a big boy. I realize it won't be easy winning your relatives over. Thing is, I'm persistent and determined."

His words along with the unrelenting glint in his eyes sent a mix of reassurance and apprehension down her spine. "They're my family. I can handle it. Let's just concentrate on keeping things as quick and low-key as possible."

"As you said, they're your family. You call the shots."

As long as she didn't try to send him packing. Then he always stepped in with more pressure for time. Well, she'd wanted to use this time to get to know each other. This driven part of him, however, she'd known from the start. What was she looking to learn by agreeing to these dates?

She wanted to know the man and Jordan kept his inner self well cloaked behind charm and smiles.

A raised voice from inside pierced through the door. Her mother was on a roll about something, not that it took much to set Bonita off anymore.

Brooke braced a palm against the stucco wall to steady herself. She should have expected this.

Were her mother's drinking and outbursts worse? Or were her own nerves simply edgier because of the pregnancy?

Jordan's hand fell from her face to grab her elbow. "Forget it. Let's blow this pop stand."

Brooke actually considered taking his suggestion until the door swung open. Brittany stood framed in the open portal. Eyes wide and frantic, she grabbed her sister by the wrist and hauled. Seemed like everyone was looking for a lifeline.

"See, Mother?" Brittany tugged her over the threshold, delicate diamond bangles jingling on her arm. "Brooke is here after all."

Her mother swayed in the archway between the living room and the hall with a crystal tumbler that could have been iced tea. Not that it ever turned out to be something so innocuous.

Her normally perfectly coiffed black hair fluffed in disarray around her face, the streaks of gray more visible than usual. For years, Lissette had helped Bonita keep up at least an air of togetherness. Apparently even their housekeeper couldn't withstand Bonita's binges that seemed to grow longer each month since her husband's death.

"Well, daughter dear, better late than never. Where were you and your... What are we supposed to call him? You're not engaged, and boyfriend doesn't sound right." She stumbled forward to lean on Brittany, her fingers clenching the glass and showing off a chipped manicure. "Isn't the current phrase baby daddy? Or do I have that backward, Brooke? You're the baby mama."

Jordan slid an arm around Brooke's waist, his jaw tight as he ushered her into the hallway. "Mrs. Garrison, Brooke and I are the parents of your grandchild."

"Of course I know that." She waved her drink in the air, sloshing some over the side to spill on the marble floor. "All of South Beach knows, thanks to that horrible media sensationalizing having children out of wedlock."

Bonita was in full form tonight. Even Jordan winced over the last comment.

Her siblings trickled from the living room into the hall with wary steps, all but Parker who plowed forward. "Mother, I think perhaps it's time for us to call it a night—"

Bonita passed her glass to her son. "Fine, here. Take it. This one's tepid anyway." She stumbled toward the stairs.

Brooke heaved a sigh of relief she heard echoed by everyone else.

Then Bonita turned, her eyes surprisingly lucid—and venomous. "It's not that I blame you, Brooke. You simply followed the pattern set by your father. Your siblings already proved that. Brittany has always run wild. And Stephen didn't even know he had a child until she was three."

Stephen parted through the press of siblings and joined Parker. "Mother, you're going too far tonight." He advanced toward his brother's side, both men grasping one of Bonita's arms to escort her with a practiced synchronicity that stung Brooke clean through. "Parker and I will help you up the stairs, and Lissette can settle you into bed."

Bonita slapped his arm away and took a step toward Brooke. "Watch yourself, young lady, or the genes will win out."

Brooke tried to force words free to stop the poison spewing from her mother's mouth, but it was all she could do to stay steady on her feet. It was mortifying enough to have Jordan view her family's awful secret, much less live it. She wouldn't disgrace herself by calling for a chair and footstool right now.

Brooke inhaled slowly, exhaled through her lips. She'd read in those pregnancy books about relaxation techniques. She found a focal point—the custom-made jeweled star topping the Christmas tree. She stared and breathed, and slowly her mother's diatribe faded to a dull blob of sounds.

Distantly she heard Jordan's voice, low, steady, with a steely edge of anger. Brooke wanted to tell her mother she would be wise to heed that steel. But the focal point wasn't staying still anymore. The darn thing was rising, and the room was growing dark.

In a brief moment of clarity, Brooke realized she was passing out just as she heard Jordan shout and felt the solid comfort of his arms catching her before she hit the floor.

* * *

So this was what fear felt like.

Jordan Jefferies had never experienced it before now, but sitting in the hospital waiting area, not knowing what was wrong with Brooke and their child, scared the hell out of him. Brooke had regained consciousness quickly enough in the car, but stayed groggy during the interminable drive to the E.R. to meet up with her obstetrician.

At least the Garrison crowd had gone stone silent since they'd all arrived at the hospital. Smart move.

Her siblings and their significant others sat along the sofas. Bonita occupied a chair by a coffeepot. The alcohol would have to work its way out of her system. For now, they had a wide-awake drunk on their hands, who at least had enough sense to shut her foul mouth.

He restrained his anger for the upset she'd caused Brooke. One look at her sent his blood simmering. How dare she talk to Brooke the way she had?

Brooke was a strong, confident force in the work world. He'd seen that in action when the Garrisons had rolled out their Sands Condominium Development project. She'd turned it into the most successful South Beach property that year, selling every last unit for record-breaking prices. He found it hard to reconcile the strength of her obvious business acumen with the softer side she gave her family.

The buzz of a pager yanked his attention back to the present. All three Garrison men reached to check their devices.

Parker winced. "Mine. Sorry. From my receptionist. Business will just have to wait."

Parker Garrison actually putting off business? A
shocker, but one Jordan was too preoccupied to
wonder at right now.

The double doors swished open and the doctor
emerged, a woman around fifty who, thank God, had
sharp eyes he would trust in a boardroom. They'd
only briefly exchanged greetings before Brooke had
been swept away into an E.R. examining room.

The doctor nodded to Parker Garrison's pregnant
wife, Anna, before turning to the whole group.
"Brooke is stable. The baby appears to be fine."

Appears? He stepped closer to the obstetrician,
wanting, needing more details, damn it. "I'm Jordan Jefferies. We didn't have a chance to speak
when Brooke came in, but I'm her fiancé and the
baby's father."

The woman nodded. "You're still not technically
a relative, but Brooke has given me the go-ahead to
speak with you. She knew you would be worried,
that her whole family would be concerned."

Worried? Understatement of the year. It was all
he could do not to blast through those double doors
to be with her.

Brittany drew up alongside him, her brothers
standing behind her in a wall of support, for once
united against something beside him. "And what's
the diagnosis?"

The physician stuffed her hands into her lab coat.

"Brooke's blood pressure is elevated, enough so that I'm ordering an overnight stay in the hospital."

His mind raced with options. None of them good. "Are you saying she has preeclampsia?"

Brittany reached out a hand to both him and Emilio at the same moment. Jordan wasn't sure if she was steadying herself or offering comfort, but he damn well couldn't bring himself to pull away.

His mind raced down daunting paths, thanks to the pregnancy and delivery books he'd read over the past week. Women who developed preeclampsia could have seizures or die. Babies could be deprived of air and nutrients to the placenta and be born with low birth weight and other complications.

The doctor relaxed her official stance and gave Jordan a sympathetic look. "Dad, stop thinking ahead and imagining those worst-case scenarios. Her problem hasn't progressed to preeclampsia as of now. We've caught this early, which is a hopeful sign. But this is definitely a warning that her body is under stress."

Stress had caused this? Of course. He'd seen firsthand the toll taken on her from family confrontation. No wonder the evening had sent her blood pressure skyrocketing.

Jordan's jaw clamped tight. This wasn't the time or place to confront Bonita Garrison, but he planned to put himself between Brooke and her family in the future. If Brooke wouldn't protect herself from them, he damn well would. "What do I need to do for her?"

"For now, I want Brooke on bed rest for a couple of weeks, low-key living and a special diet." She gave his arm another pat. "Hang in there, Dad, you can come back to her room and see her in about five minutes. She's been asking for you."

Brooke wanted to see him? Thank God he wouldn't have to figure out how to angle his way into the place where he needed to be most right now. Relief rattled through him so intensely, he barely noticed the doctor leaving and Bonita sobbing her way toward the ladies' bathroom.

Five minutes and he could see Brooke. Jordan swallowed hard and wondered how one willowy woman and a barely formed baby could knock the ground out from under him in a way nothing else had before.

He didn't like this feeling one damn bit.

When he looked up from the ugly tile floor, he realized that he wasn't alone. Emilio stood silently on one side. And what the hell? Parker waited on the other, his black eye from their fight still not fully faded.

Jordan stared at the line of Garrison offspring and while they unquestionably loved Brooke, he didn't trust they could keep her safe from Bonita's talons. There was only one way he could make sure Brooke had total peace and her every need met. "I'm taking Brooke home with me."

Her brother Adam quirked a brow. "Isn't that for her to decide?"

Jordan planted his feet and his resolve. "Like any of you would handle the situation differently if you were in my shoes."

He watched her three brothers wince with chagrin, then resolution as they glanced at the women beside them. Her brothers might be his adversaries in the Jefferies-Garrison war for power, but they certainly shared the same drive.

Emilio grinned. "Good luck convincing her without upsetting her, bro."

And thank God for brothers who could wrench a much-needed laugh out at just the right time. Emilio gave him a quick, hard hug and stepped away to comfort his fiancée, leaving Parker still standing beside him.

"You care about my sister," Parker said, the words sounding more like a statement than a question.

Jordan gave a simple nod. More and more every day. More than he'd expected or knew how to take in.

Parker sighed long, hard. "Okay, then. We'll gather up Mother and head out. Let Brooke know how worried we are for her and the baby."

Jordan glanced toward the ladies' restroom with no sign of Bonita yet. Still he kept his voice low, but level. "About Bonita. Normally I make it a point to stay out of other people's family affairs, but Brooke and our child are my family now."

Parker frowned. "Your point?"

This wouldn't be easy to say or hear, but after a night like this, he couldn't keep quiet. Especially when Brooke needed his help. "It seems to me that hiding the liquor bottles isn't working anymore."

Jordan waited for the explosion, a fist or at the very least a bark to mind his own business. Yet none came.

Only a heavy resolution in the air as the eldest Garrison nodded. "I'll look into inpatient rehab clinics first thing in the morning."

No victory here. Just a hard truth. Jordan kept his silence.

Parker sagged back against the wall. "I'm certain the brothers will be on board to join me in an intervention for Mother. Brittany's probably going to want to stay with Brooke." He looked back at his siblings and all nodded in agreement, Brittany swiping at a tear streaking down her face. Parker turned back to Jordan. "We'll let you know how it goes."

A few short words exchanged, but enough. They'd been adversaries for a long time. Working together didn't—and wouldn't—come easy. But given Emilio's marriage and this baby, their families would have to get along.

Bonita was a destructive force to those around her, and he wanted better for Brooke and their child.

Speaking of which, now he just had to figure out a diplomatic way to persuade her to move in with him, without raising anyone's blood pressure. That would most definitely take a Christmas miracle.

Eight

Brooke let the soft leather of the limo seat envelop her, her feet propped up and a water bottle clasped in her hand. Jordan sprawled beside her, working away on his BlackBerry.

Hot.

Silent.

And always present during her every waking moment in the hospital.

She kept her other hand pressed to her stomach to reassure herself the baby still rested safely inside her. The smell of the hospital and fear clung to her senses even miles away. Everything had happened so quickly, from passing out to waking in Jordan's car as they raced to the E.R.

Now the world had slowed, in every sense. She couldn't work. Couldn't go anywhere. The helplessness pinched, but she didn't have a choice. Already maternal instincts to protect this precious life burned so strongly. She would do whatever it took to keep her child safe.

Although so far, she hadn't needed to do much beyond dress herself. Jordan had taken care of everything, checking her out of the hospital and whisking her away in the limo. However, when she got to her place, she would regain some control. Her assistant could bring any pressing work over, and Lissette's niece had been looking for part-time employment. With someone who could help during the day, she should be fine.

She could do some paperwork at home to keep from going stir-crazy. Parker had even offered to send over his receptionist, Sheila, to take care of business errands, but Brooke reassured him her staff at the Sands could handle things.

One morning off work, and already she was going stir-crazy. She needed to calm herself, for the baby's sake.

Brooke stared out the limo window, counting palm trees whipping by to steady her thoughts...as they passed the exit to her condo. "Hey, we missed the turnoff to my place."

Jordan glanced up, tucked his BlackBerry in his briefcase on the seat beside him and focused the full attention of those yummy blue eyes on her. "I know.

I didn't want to give you time to stress about this. Stressing isn't good for you or the baby."

"Stress about what?" Was the doctor keeping something from her? Her fingers curved around her stomach.

Jordan stretched his arm along the back of her seat. "I'm going to take care of you."

Ah, now she saw the way this was going. "You're using this as an excuse for us to move in together. I don't want to stay in a hotel room for weeks on end."

"Not at the Victoria." He toyed with her hair, loose around her shoulders. "At my house, with a full staff to wait on you while you stay on bed rest."

"Your house?"

"Yes, or actually my parents' old home, but mine now. I bought out Emilio's half a long while back."

He lived in his parents' old house? The notion teased at her heart, thinking of him wanting to stay close to memories of his mother and father. If only he would show this softer side of himself to her more often.

It was his charge-ahead side she had to worry about. She forced her attention back to what he was saying.

"You can't take care of yourself alone at your place, Brooke, you have to know that. Do you want me to move into your pink palace? Or would you rather go home with someone in your family taking care of you?"

The thought of staying at the Garrison estate

with her mother… "That's dirty pool for a guy who swears he doesn't want to piss me off."

"I'm simply showing you the options." His fingers tunneled through her hair to massage her neck, tease her senses. "Do you have a better idea?"

Brittany was getting ready for her wedding, even more so now that she wouldn't have Brooke's help. And she didn't really know her sisters-in-law well enough to be comfortable living with them, even as nice as they were. All of her female friends worked full-time, living alone in a condo like she did. "I thought I could hire someone."

"I've already got a full staff taking care of the house." His thumb worked along her spine in muscle-melting strokes. "Think of it this way. Since our dates out on the town have been curbed for now, we can have the same sort of getting-to-know-each-other time at my home. More efficiently."

She stared out the limo window as they drove deeper into South Beach with each palm tree that whipped past. Rollerbladers zipped along the sidewalks despite the cooler temperatures. Tourists filled crosswalks, the older contingent moving in for the winter months.

His argument had merit. Still, she wondered if he harbored further ulterior motives. "I can't have sex until the doctor clears me."

"She warned me again in the hall." He winced. "Stringently."

She grinned at just the thought of that conversation. "Not much privacy in this baby-birthing pro-cess, is there?"

"Apparently not." He rested his head against the side of her forehead, nuzzling her hair. "I'll miss being with you more than I can say. But if you can go without sex, so can I."

No sex. Already she mourned the loss. With Jordan touching her, she couldn't deny how uncomfortable holding back might get. "You're really serious about us moving in together, temporarily anyway."

She let the implications rain down around her, this new facet of Jordan's commitment to her. She had been watching him for any false moves, any sign that he was in this relationship with ulterior motives or to somehow bring down the Garrison empire. But his tenderness and thoughtful gene-rosity now... She couldn't deny that she was moved.

"Totally. And if you can't consider your own health, think about the baby."

Of course, Jordan being Jordan, now he was really playing dirty pool. Except he'd hit on the one argument guaranteed to sway her. "For the baby, but I need to set some ground rules."

"Fair enough." He stared at her with those board-room blue eyes, his make-the-best-deal-possible eyes.

"And you have to *promise* to follow them."

"You're good at catching nuances." He winked, humor easing his intensity. "I've heard you're as tough as the rest of your family across the bargain-ing table."

"Another dubious compliment." Although she had to admit, while a peacemaker in personal relationships, she enjoyed releasing her suppressed aggressions in the workplace. "But on to those rules. Just because I gave in on this doesn't mean I'm relenting on my reservations about marriage."

The notion still scared her to pieces, and she didn't plan on thinking about anything that would stress her out.

"Understood."

"And I think it's best if we don't share a bed." She figured she should cover all the nuances he may have tried to sneak past her.

His eyes crinkled at the corners as his smile increased. "Because you're afraid you can't resist me?"

"That's quite an ego you're sporting."

"Or sense of humor." He grazed her lips with his thumb. "I'm trying to make you smile back."

His gentle touch stroked her scattered emotions. "Sorry. I'm just…scared."

All levity faded from his gaze, and he slid his hand to cup her face. "Ah, damn, of course you are."

"I could handle it if this was just about my health, but worrying about the baby, that's too much." The concerns bubbling inside her were so much bigger than anything she'd ever faced.

"Worry is against doctor's orders." He smoothed his other hand over her stomach in a gesture of intimacy she couldn't bring herself to stop. "Set your mind on something else."

She blinked through the fears, accepting he was right, knowing she needed to try harder for their baby's sake. "Such as?"

"Have you thought about names?"

The limo stopped at a light while hordes of pedestrian traffic crossed the street. She let herself settle into the warmth of his touch and the butter-soft leather seats as they shared the moment, planning together for their child. "It would have helped if the little one had been more cooperative during all those ultrasounds. Then we could have known whether to choose girl or boy names."

"We?"

He'd doubted she would include him? Further proof he didn't know her well if he thought she could be so small-minded as to cut him out of such a huge decision about their baby. "Of course, you should get a say in this, unless you come up with something horrid. What's your mother's name?"

"Victoria."

"Your hotel's name," she murmured in surprise. How could she not have known that? Yet another reminder of how far they needed to come before she could even consider tying her life—and the knot— with this man.

He shrugged.

"That's really touching." She wanted the same sort of closeness with her own child, something better than her relationship with Bonita. "I'm sorry about how my mother behaved earlier."

His eyes took on that sharp look again. Predatory, unrelenting. "You have nothing to apologize for."

She still felt guilty for not thinking through her actions more that night five months ago. "The first time I took you to dinner, my brother beat you up—"

"Uh, you mean *tried* to beat me up."

Male egos. She stifled a laugh. "Right," she said, then sobered. "Anyway, and the next time we showed up at my house, my *mother* goes on the attack, verbally rather than physically."

"You were the one who was hurt. I should have stepped in sooner."

As if that would have made a difference. Her hands shaking, she set aside her water bottle. "No one can stop her when she's on a roll like that."

However, she needed to stop her mother in the future since there was no way she could allow Bonita to jeopardize this baby's health. Anger stirred at what her mother's tirade had nearly cost them.

He rested a hand on top of her clenched fist. "I don't think this is a wise discussion for you to be having."

"Think happy thoughts and all." She forced even breaths in, out, in again.

"Exactly." He raised her hand to his mouth and grazed a kiss across her knuckles, once, twice and again until her fist unfurled and the gold band on her thumb appeared again. "Tell me a *happy* childhood memory."

She offered up the first thing that popped to mind. "My mother used to paint. She would take her art supplies to the beach. Brittany and I could build sand castles and splash in the waves."

"That's a great memory." He thumbed along the inside of her wrist as the limo pulled up to the iron gates outside his family home on the north end of the strip.

"I hadn't thought about it in such a long time. The bad memories tend to overtake the good ones." She eyed the opening gates, envisioning them closing behind her. Closing her in with the manicured bushes and trees. "I guess you and I need to make sure those bad feelings between our families don't overcome the good stuff we're working on."

He studied her as the limo rolled along the brick paved driveway, past a fountain with an angel in the center. "I agree, as long as thinking about that doesn't stress you."

"Hmm… If I was a Machiavellian type of person, I could really milk this to my advantage and pick the name I want."

"As long as we don't have to name the kid Parker, I think I can handle just about anything."

Much-needed laughter rolled up and past her lips. She clapped a hand over her mouth. "I'll think about names and get back to you."

"Fair enough." He winked on his way out of the limo.

Before she even reached the walkway, he swept her into his arms. She started to argue, but they'd already been down this route and he seemed insistent on carrying her. Today, at least, she had a valid reason to accept the ride without worry of losing control of the situation.

She looped her arms around his neck as he took the stone steps and wound his way through a columned courtyard to the front door. She barely had time to take in the warm honey-and-blue hues of his home since he introduced her to the staff in a quick flurry before heading toward the lengthy staircase with a deep mahogany railing curling around the foyer.

The long hall seemed narrower because of the framed artwork. Landscapes mingled with portraits of a heart-tuggingly young Jordan, as well as Emilio. Already, she could feel her eyes drifting closed as much as she wanted to stay awake and look around at this slice of family-centered heaven that was his home. Doggone it, these pregnancy near-narcoleptic moments seemed to hit her harder every day.

The world shifted, and she blinked awake again as he settled her in the middle of a towering four-poster bed. Jordan wafted the fluffy duvet over her with cocooning comfort—and then the first hints of claustrophobia. It only took her one sweep of the room to realize…

She wasn't in his bed, but she was most definitely in his suite.

A week later, Jordan took the stairs in his house up to the second floor with anticipation. He had food and a present for Brooke, both of which he thought would lift her spirits.

No question, he enjoyed having her under his roof more than even he'd anticipated. He'd brought her here because it was the right thing to do for her and the child.

He hadn't expected it to be so right for him, too.

Especially after living alone for such a long time, sometimes at the hotel, sometimes here. The bachelor life had suited his career aspirations well. He'd envisioned there being more of a pinch in adding her to his routine. Instead, the past days had been entertaining, spent sharing meals, talking, learning the fundamentals about each other. Her favorite color, food, music.

Pink—no surprise.

Chili—for now. Subject to hormonal change.

Oldies and soft rock—he had a concert in mind for when she was on her feet again.

He hoped that would be soon, for the baby's safety as well as her sanity. He couldn't miss the restlessness growing in Brooke with each passing day. He'd done his best to keep her occupied, sending in contractors to renovate a bedroom into a nursery when she wasn't tackling some work from her office. He hadn't met a woman yet who wasn't thrilled at the prospect of a bottomless budget for decorating.

Except Brooke didn't seem the least bit thrilled tonight, lying on the sofa in the sitting area be-

tween their rooms. She appeared downright ir-
ritable staring at her feet propped on a pillow at the
other end of the sofa. Her fax machine hummed
quietly on the far side of the room even though she
didn't so much as glance at the papers spewing out
in her work area.

He stepped into the room, rested the wrapped
package against the couch and placed the carryout
container on the coffee table—none of which
elicited any reaction from her. "Brooke? Don't you
want supper from Emilio's? There's a container of
chili in here with your name on it." Even the mention of one of her favorite foods didn't change the
weariness on her face. "We can order something
else, if you're having a different craving."

She shook her head. "No. That's fine. Thanks."

He swept aside the pillow and rested her feet in
his lap. He savored the chance to touch her, look at
her. Her simple red cotton dress clung to the luscious curves of her breasts and to her stomach, the
increasing swell a reminder of how little time he had
left to cement things between them. He'd always
hoped for a marriage like his parents', and this pregnancy had prevented him from finding that with
Brooke. Yet. He could still hope they would find that
magic, but only if they both tried.

As much as he wanted to tunnel his hands under
her dress for unfettered access to her, he limited
himself to stroking no higher than her knees. Two
minutes into the massage, she still hadn't relaxed.

What the hell? "All right, I'm stumped. What gives?"

"It's all this." She swept her hand to encompass the stacks of wallpaper books and paint samples.

"Baby preparations? I told the contractor and interior designer to let you pick whatever you want."

She swung her feet off his lap. "But you're picking decorators and knocking out walls and trying to take over my life."

Okay. At least she'd been honest, not that he understood her in the least. What was he supposed to do? Back away?

However, he couldn't fight with her, even if the doctor had reassured them she was rapidly improving. Her blood pressure was already down to normal. A few more days with her feet up, just to be safe, and she would be cleared in time for Brittany's wedding.

Still, he wasn't taking any chances by arguing with her. "Regardless of whether or not you live here, I need to set up a place for the baby. I would like your input. If you end up living here, great. Regardless, it will give you something to do while you sit around. I know you've decreased your workload, and I thought this would fill the gap with something lighter."

"I figured I could still help with my sister's wedding through phone calls."

"I'm cool with whatever doesn't stress you out."

Her brown eyes snapped with irritation. "You're not the one with the final say in that."

Damn. He wanted her to quit veiling her thoughts from him, and he'd sure gotten his wish today. No doubt about where she stood on that issue.

Unfortunately, he'd been having the final say on most everything in his life for a long time. He took a deep breath and tried to be patient.

"I worry you don't know when to stop pushing yourself. I know you're bored."

"Bored is too mild a word. If my family didn't visit, I would go nuts." Her head fell back with a heavy sigh. "Although I'm starting to wonder if you've locked Mother out of the front gate. I really expected she would show up by now, not that I'm complaining about her absence after our last encounter."

He started to lead the conversation in another, less stressful direction, then changed his mind. Bottled-up stress was worse, according to her doctor. "How long has she been an alcoholic?"

"For as long as I can remember. Even when she painted on the beach, the jug of sangria went along with her." She looked down from the ceiling to meet his eyes. "It's not like we were neglected. We always had round-the-clock nannies—and each other."

"That doesn't negate what your mother put you through."

"I know."

He stared in her eyes and saw the milky-brown darken with frustration, pain, then helplessness. Her siblings had wanted to keep the news of Bonita entering rehab from Brooke. Jordan realized now that she should know. He would face the wrath of the Garrisons, if need be.

Jordan thought about reaching for her hand, but she still had those stand-back vibes going. "Your brothers met with your mother to discuss her problem."

"They did what?" Her eyebrows rose in surprise, before slamming down again. "Wait… You knew and you didn't tell me?"

"Do you really think you could have participated in an intervention in your condition right now?"

"Okay, fair enough." Her stiff spine eased. "What happened?"

"They checked your mother into a rehab center the day you were released from the hospital." How would Brooke feel about that? He couldn't get a read off her. "Are you okay with this?"

"Of course. It's a good thing. I just can't help but feel I should have been there." She took his hand, the distance between them fading for the moment. "Thank you for telling me, though. I understand you're trying to pamper me, but I can't take your keeping things from me. There have been too many secrets in my family. If I found out you were lying to me…"

He felt her slender fingers curl around his, understood the gesture she'd made in reaching out to him. Now he faced another dilemma. Tell her the truth about what he'd done with the newspaper leak and risk everything. Or roll the dice that she would never find out.

Damn it. He knew what he had to do. "I need to tell you something."

"Hey, why the scowl? It can't be worse than having to think about my mother in rehab."

"This honesty stuff, I want to be straight up with you."

Her delicately arched eyebrows pinched together. "You're starting to scare me, and that's not good."

"Then I'll just spill it. The newspaper leak about our relationship wasn't an accident."

Her hand went ice-cold in his.

She eased her fingers free. "You started the media frenzy?"

He hadn't meant to stir all the gossip about her family, but that was beside the point. It was his fault, and he took full responsibility for the strain he could now see it had placed on Brooke. "I'm not going to make excuses for my behavior. All I can say is that I would do things differently now, and I'm sorry."

Brooke hugged her stomach protectively for another long stretch of time before nodding. "You wanted to get the announcement over with all at once."

"What makes you think that?" He'd expected anger, tears even, but not an understanding of his motives. He'd always prided himself on playing things close to the vest. What people didn't know they couldn't use against him.

Having someone see through him so thoroughly was uncomfortable.

She shrugged. "That's what Parker would do, and you two are a lot alike."

Well that bit. Hard. "You're that mad at me, are you?"

"I'm disappointed, but I understand. But you have to realize that when you make unilateral decisions that affect both of us—without telling me—you're not easing stress for me. You're increasing it, especially after the passive way I've handled family relationships for too long. Whether I sense something's off or find out later, it tears at me."

Guilt hammered at him, made all the worse by how easily she'd let him off the hook, even going so far as to take some responsibility by mentioning how she'd dealt with her family in the past. *I'm sorry* seemed too little to offer.

"I won't excuse what you did, Jordan, but I can see where you came to your decision and forgive what happened." Her spine straightened with unmistakable steel. "As long as you promise never to lie to me again."

"That, I can do." And he meant it. He was ambitious, even had a reputation for being ruthless—which he wouldn't deny—but he prided himself on honesty. No question, the newspaper thing hadn't been one of his wiser moves, hindsight. "Are you ready for supper?"

She inched away from him and stood in an unmistakable back-off message. "As long as we're being open with each other, I need some space tonight."

She hesitated and he thought—hoped—she might relent. She reached toward him…

And snagged the carryout bag of food before turning back to her bedroom.

Not bothering to stifle his grin at her accepting at least one of his gifts, he watched Brooke walk away and disappear behind her door. He wanted to follow her, but would leave her alone and let her sleep. Rest was the best thing for her and the baby. For tonight, he figured he'd wrangled more forgiveness than expected.

However, he hadn't figured on being so damn disappointed at the missed opportunity to share chili and a movie with Brooke.

Brooke wrestled with sleep and the covers, the confrontation with Jordan leaving her frustrated and restless.

She stared at the clock—2:00 a.m. She'd seen midnight, as well, but must have drifted off.

God, she hated this helpless feeling of losing control of her life. Her family had staged an intervention with her mother, a huge, life-changing moment.

While Brooke sat around with her feet propped up, unable to handle stress. No wonder Brittany had been so edgy when she'd come to visit after Brooke left the hospital. The whole family must have gone through hell, and yet they'd all continued to tiptoe around her. Doing the right thing wasn't necessarily easy.

Why couldn't Jordan have told her sooner? Her

mother seeking help was a good thing, the right thing. Hope warred with skepticism.

And therein lay her main problem, trusting that her mother would make it through the program successfully. Trusting, after a lifetime of mixed signals from her parents.

Trusting Jordan.

Even with their dates and living together this past week, it still seemed like too little time to know each other before committing to marriage. Her parents had dated for two years before marrying and look how that had turned out.

If only she could recapture—and trust—that intense sense of rightness she'd felt the night she'd decided to sleep with him for the first time.

The night they'd made this baby...

She'd seen him many times. She'd always wanted him.

Tonight, her family be damned, she would have him.

The decision echoed in her mind all the way up the elevator to the room she'd secured for herself and Jordan Jefferies.

Her head spun more from the touch of his hands on her body than from any effects of alcohol. She'd felt the attraction between them for years, but never imagined the sparks would combust through her with such intensity.

His palms, sweeping down her back during their frantic kiss down the hall.

His palms, cupping her bottom to pull her closer as they stumbled through the door.

His fingers, making fast work of her clothes in order to torment her.

And even when she demanded her place on top, still those talented hands teased her senses to the edge of fulfillment. Stopping short. Taking her to the brink and back again until they both tumbled over in a tangle of arms and legs and uncontained cries…

Brooke woke with the sheet twisted around her ankles, her body achy with want for what she'd experienced with him, an intense completion remembered in her dream.

Yet she hadn't found the same relief tonight.

She reached to click on her bedside lamp. As always, there waited a pitcher of water along with fresh fruit for a late-night snack. She snagged a pear and crunched. If she couldn't satisfy her sexual hunger, she would settle for feeding another appetite.

What was it about that time with Jordan that haunted her so? A sense of control in that moment, of equality. Except by the morning after she'd felt so *out* of control, she'd run from him, was running still.

Her eyes gravitated to the open door. Jordan must have checked on her after she went to sleep and then left the door open. She stared through at the books of fabric samples resting by the small sofa in the sitting room. He'd given her choices, but that didn't stop her from feeling smothered.

She glanced away only to see a blue wrapped

package propped along the edge of the couch. Vaguely, she recalled Jordan had been carrying something—that—when he'd entered the room. So he'd bought her a present to win her over.

She munched on the pear and studied the gift with trepidation. With the dream having left her pensive and vulnerable, she wasn't sure she could take more of Jordan tonight.

But curiosity nipped and nibbled.

Tossing the rest of the pear into the trash can, she kicked free of the sheet and swung her feet to the floor. Her satiny nightshirt slithered over her skin in a sensual caress that reminded her all too well of her dream, of the real-life night that had been anything but a dream, yet most definitely fantasy material.

She padded across the room and sat on the edge of the sofa. Her fingers fell to rest on the top of the gift and tapped restlessly. If only she had her impulsive twin here to help her decide what to do next.

Memories of childhood Christmases shuffled through, of Brittany picking up each wrapped present, touching it, shaking it, then confidently proclaiming what she suspected it contained. Fifty percent of the time, Brittany was right. The other half, her guesses were so deliberately outrageous, no one bothered to tease her over being wrong.

Brooke stared at the package. Not jewelry. Not clothes. Too big to be a photo album. Too small to be furniture, even unassembled.

Finally, curiosity won out over caution. She tugged

the present around and began tearing the blue-striped paper away to find—bubble wrap. Lots and lots of bubble wrap protecting something underneath. No wonder she'd been unable to hazard a guess.

She ripped at the tape securing the covering. She slowly realized some kind of framed artwork was inside. He'd bought her a picture? Or a painting?

Without question, he was showering her with attention. He *was* trying. But she didn't want to start off their relationship with the notion that she could be purchased. A last swipe cleared away the plastic…

And stole her breath.

He hadn't bought her some exotic piece of art. Instead he'd chosen a watercolor—obviously meant for a nursery—of two little girls playing on the beach, making sand castles.

Jordan remembered her telling him about the happy memory from her childhood.

The thoughtfulness of his gift touched her as firmly as his hands ever had. *This* side of Jordan she simply couldn't resist. Not tonight with the dream still teasing at the corners of her mind, not with an ache of loneliness and yearning for more stirring inside her.

Resting the painting carefully along the sofa, Brooke stood, her eyes and intentions firmly planted on the connecting door leading to Jordan's bedroom.

Nine

Jordan woke the moment he heard his door hinges creak.

He held still, watching through narrowly open eyes as Brooke made her way across the room toward him. Even in the near pitch-dark he could see she was not in any distress, so he kept his silence, biding his time to discover what she had in mind. He never knew anymore around her, and that bothered him.

She stopped by his bed, seemingly unaware that he continued to study her through the veil of his eyelashes. She plucked at the edge of the covers.

Holy crap. She couldn't be about to…

Brooke slid in beside him. He couldn't stop the

rush of air gusting from his lungs any more than he could contain himself from reaching to wrap an arm around her. The flowery scent of her hair teased his nose as she snuggled against him.

"Trouble sleeping?" he asked. His hand slid to her stomach and began rubbing soothing circles. "Is the future soccer star kicking you awake?"

Bad idea, touching her. Especially when this could lead nowhere.

She settled alongside him, her head resting on his shoulder. "Something woke me up. Not the baby though."

"Can I get you anything?" He smoothed his hand from her belly to her back. He'd noticed she'd begun pressing a hand to her lower spine over the past week.

"I needed to be with you." She flattened her palm to his chest.

His body tightened in response to her cool fingers on his overheated flesh. The rasp from the ring on her thumb seared along his skin, and what a time to think of how he could envision the vine pattern etched on the ring. He'd come to know her that well.

He clenched his jaw and started counting backward from one hundred. By seventy-eight, he gave up and accepted that he would simply have to live with the pain. "Okay, if you want to sleep in here, no way am I going to object."

He continued the back massage, a mix of heaven and hell to have her in his arms, feel her soft curves against him, under his hands. He reminded himself that if he kept himself in check and won her over, he could be with her again. The opportunity to have his child raised by the two of them together was worth any wait.

And the idea of a life with Brooke grew more appealing the longer they spent together.

She stroked along his ear. "I don't feel much like sleeping."

Neither did he, but for a different reason. He focused on the click of the ceiling fan overhead, the white noise helping keep him grounded. "Then we'll talk." She'd said something earlier about resenting feeling controlled, so he opted for a more neutral question. "What would you like to do tomorrow after I get home from work?"

"I wish we could go to all the parties for Brittany and Emilio this week."

No wonder she was restless. "I'm so damn sorry. Being stuck in the house must be boring. What do you say we check with the doctor about going for a drive along the shore? As long as we don't travel far and you're not walking around, I'll bet it's all right. We can take a limo so you can prop your feet."

"That would be nice," she answered with zilch in the way of enthusiasm.

Ah, damn. He remembered she wanted to make decisions, too… "Any other ideas?"

She sighed. "I don't mean to sound cranky. That really is thoughtful, like the beautiful present you bought."

So she'd finally opened it. He had to admit he'd been disappointed when their argument had forestalled him giving it to her. At least he had the satisfaction of knowing she appreciated the gift. After purchasing it, he'd wondered if perhaps she might prefer a chunky diamond bracelet instead—as the other women he'd dated would have. Without question, his last ex would have preferred diamonds over any painting.

He needed to remember Brooke wasn't even similar to any other woman.

"I'm glad you liked it. When I saw it in the gallery window, I had a feeling you might." And how strange that he found himself seeing Brooke in any number of things he came across in the course of a day.

"I unwrapped it after I woke up." She cuddled nearer, her knee nestling too damn close between his legs. "I was dreaming of you."

"I'm glad." He dreamed about her every night, a notion that sent him throbbing against the gentle pressure of her thigh.

Hey, wait. She couldn't mean her dream in the same way as his…?

Her hand skimmed over his hip.

Damn.

He grasped her wrist. "Brooke, honey, as much as I enjoy touching you and you touching me, we can't have sex. Not until your doctor clears you."

"I know. I just needed…" She shrugged, her body grazing against his and sending the satiny fabric of her nightshirt slithering over his chest in a tempting whisper. "I wanted to thank you for the painting you bought for the nursery."

Jordan allowed himself the satisfaction of toying with her hair. "You're welcome."

"And I'm sorry I was crabby earlier. It really is tough for me, sitting around all the time."

She settled her head against his shoulder with a sigh that pressed her breasts against his hot flesh. He welcomed her ease with their closeness, even as her sweet curves tempted him.

He would definitely have to call the doctor about a limo ride for Brooke. The doctor had said Brooke was doing well. She might soon be moving back to her condo…away from him.

Jordan brushed aside thoughts of time ticking down for them and focused on her current frustration. "I'll talk to your family about visiting more."

"They're visiting plenty." She scrunched her nose. "I've talked to people until I'm blue in the face. I'm restless. I need…you. This."

So did he. He stroked her back again, tried to calm her to sleep before they both lost their freaking minds. "Shh. Relax."

He could feel all the tensed muscles knotting along her shoulders. She truly did need to relax. Being this edgy couldn't be good for her. If only he could take care of her sensual needs without having sex—

Inspiration lit. He smiled, the thrill of what he *could* do for her sending a rush through him.

He cut the restraints and let his hands roam freely to her breasts, lush from carrying his child. Her response was immediate and gratifying as she moaned, arching into his palms.

Her eyes drifted closed, her panting breaths pushing her against his hands again and again. "Jordan, the no-sex problem. Remember?"

"I remember." He would never do anything to risk her health or that of their child. Sure he wanted her, but he was man enough to wait for his own gratification. "We're not going to have sex. I'm just going to help you feel less…restless."

His hand slid to her hip to caress high and higher still on her thigh. "If that's what you want."

She edged closer, guiding his fingers. "I definitely want, but what about you?"

"We can worry about me another time." He tucked a finger inside the band of her low-cut panties and rubbed along the smooth skin of her stomach. "Tonight's about you."

He covered her mouth with his while sweeping away her underwear. Sighing into his kiss, she kicked free the scrap of satin. He sought, found, the tight bud between her legs. His thumb teased back and forth, eliciting another happy hum from her. As much as he wanted to watch her face, he enjoyed kissing her too damn much to stop, took pleasure in the feel of her frantic hands grasping at his shoulders, her fingernails digging into his skin.

Soon, sooner than he'd expected, her chest rose

and fell rapidly. She moaned repeated don't-stop urgings as she pressed more firmly against him. The speed of her response to his touch surged through him. He opened his eyes to take in the beauty of her face as she found her release, her grip digging deeper into him.

Three gasps later, she sagged onto her back, her head burrowing into her pillow. Puffy breaths slid between her lips. And yeah, he took plenty of satisfaction in knowing how much he affected her. He might have transferred a boatload of her restlessness to himself, but it pleased him no end to see the way she relaxed into his arms now, her cheeks still flushed and her mouth swollen from his kiss.

"Better?" he asked, unable to take his eyes off her.

She smiled slowly. "Much."

He gathered her close until she settled with a final sigh. He stroked her hair away from her face while she relaxed against him, her breathing evening out with sleep.

"Good night, beautiful," he whispered against her hair.

He knew how right it was for her to be in his bed. Why couldn't she understand it, as well? As much as he wanted to take reassurance from her presence here, from her joy over the painting, he couldn't forget their argument earlier. He'd never met anyone as stubborn as Brooke in a quiet, determined way that crept up on a person.

Jordan glanced at the clock—4:00 a.m.

He knew without question sleep wouldn't be coming to him as easily as it had for Brooke.

It would be a long three days until her next visit to the doctor.

Brooke settled in the back of the limo after her OB appointment and allowed herself the huge sigh of relief she'd kept restrained at the clinic.

Thank goodness she could do away with being chauffeured around now that the doctor had cleared her. All looked good with the baby and her blood pressure. She wished Jordan could have been there with her—knew he wanted to be—but he'd been stuck in traffic blocked off by an accident. He'd called once the wreck was cleared, but she'd already been on her way back to the exam room. There simply wasn't time for Jordan to make it across town to meet her.

At least she could surprise him with all the good news—and an ultrasound photo of their son.

A baby boy.

She let images of playing on the beach with her little one stir in her head. She allowed those dreams to shift with Jordan stepping into the scenario. For the first time she could imagine a future with him, a happily-ever-after where they let love grow between them.

Love.

The word still gave her heart an uncomfortable squeeze, but she waited through it rather than shying away as she'd done in the past.

She concentrated on all the good news she would share with him soon. Not only was she okay to attend her sister's wedding and return to work, but she'd been cleared by her doctor to resume *all* normal activities.

Including sex.

After their steamy encounter the night of her dream, they'd begun sharing a bed, a tormenting pleasure. She'd wanted more during those nights, yet took comfort in the strength of his arms. Without question, she slept better with him at her side.

Tonight, they wouldn't sleep, not for a long while, anyway.

And tomorrow? She would worry about that in the morning. Because right now, she couldn't think of anything other than making tracks to locate Jordan and find the nearest bed. Lucky for them both, the Hotel Victoria offered plenty of options.

Jordan glanced at the time on his computer screen, wishing he was with Brooke rather than at the Hotel Victoria. He would have been if not for the traffic jam on the causeway that had eventually sent him back to his desk.

He wanted to find Brooke and hear about her visit to the doctor. He'd tried to call her, but she wasn't picking up her phone.

He glanced at his clock again. What was keeping her? Memories of that terrible night in the E.R. tormented him. He shoved up from his chair, ready to start checking the roads if she didn't show up soon. Maybe he'd misunderstood her earlier, and she'd simply gone to his house.

Jordan reached for the phone to call his house-keeper just as the door began to open.

Relief socked him. Dead center. "Brooke—"

Except the woman in the doorway wasn't the mother of his child. Instead, he found the last person he expected—or wanted—to see right now.

His ex-lover, Sheila McKay.

He put up his guard as fast as he rose to his feet. She'd been persistent the past few weeks, trying to get in touch with him. Apparently she didn't accept rejection easily. "Sheila, my assistant shouldn't have let you up here."

He'd tried to be calm and civil when he'd stopped dating Sheila over six months ago, but she'd con-tinually attempted to jump-start their relationship. Shortly after he had broken up with her, she'd taken a job as a receptionist at Garrison Inc.—and promptly worked to lure him back with valuable insider information.

Sheila sashayed into his work area on spiky high heels. "Your assistant must be taking a coffee break, because I didn't see anyone except a few whistling construction workers."

How in the world had he ever found this con-ceited woman attractive? Her blond hair, blue eyes and Playboy bunny history didn't matter. She paled in comparison to Brooke.

He glanced at his watch pointedly. "This isn't a good time. I'm on my way out. I'll escort you to your car."

Sheila perched a hip on his desk, unmistakably encroaching on his personal space. "It'll be worth your while to wait. I have some pretty interesting inside scoop from the Garrison camp on some stock purchasing plans."

There had been a time he and Emilio accepted any tidbits on the Garrisons she offered. That time had passed. He'd promised Brooke honesty and he meant to follow through on that vow.

He thought he'd been clear with Sheila in their last phone conversation that they were done. And when she'd persisted by leaving messages, he'd made his point again with silence. Apparently subtlety didn't work with her. "Sheila, I'm not in the market for any information you have about the Garrisons. If you've even glanced at the newspapers, you know I'm committed to Brooke now. Besides, any relationship you and I had ended months ago."

"Oh, that's right." She shrugged her long hair over her shoulder. "You have your own in with that family now."

His jaw tightened over the notion of gossip like that upsetting Brooke. "Watch yourself, Sheila. You're overstepping."

He rounded the desk, set on ushering Sheila out—and away from *his* files—on his way down to the car.

"I need to get home to Brooke. She had a visit to the doctor today, and I want to hear how it went."

Sheila stepped in front of him, blocking the pathway to the door. "It must be tough for you, having her on bed rest."

Why hadn't he seen through this woman from the start? An image of them as a couple flashed through his mind. He winced inwardly at the memory of himself then, the kind of man who didn't always take the time to see beyond the surface when it came to bed partners.

Then nearly six months ago, Brooke had blazed into his life with so much more than surface attraction. The heat had transformed him into something different, someone he liked a whole lot more. That knowledge made it ridiculously easy to push this superficially beautiful woman away from him. "It's tougher for her with the cabin fever, which is why I'm leaving now."

"I imagine a strong man like you is experiencing a different fever altogether." Her painted lips curved in a knowing smile.

Enough wasting time. He cut straight to the chase. "Sheila, I'm committed to making a future with Brooke and our child."

"So? I'm not looking for a serious relationship. That doesn't mean we can't have fun." She reached to cup his neck. "You look like you need to let go and relax."

Her touch left him cold. No surprise. He gripped

her arms, ready to move her gently, but firmly, away. "Sheila, it's time for you to go—"

A gasp stopped him midsentence.

Damn it. He knew before he looked. Brooke had made it back from her appointment.

Tears clouding her vision, Brooke jabbed the elevator's down button again and again. Sure, it didn't make the thing arrive any faster, but the action provided an outlet for her anger—and disillusionment.

A traffic jam?

She'd been an idiot to believe his lame excuse. She couldn't help but think of how often she'd seen a similar scenario play out with her parents. Her father would always offer an excuse as to why he couldn't spend more time at home. Her mother would cry—then drink.

Now Brooke knew all too well what her father had been doing during the time away. Seeing his other family. She wouldn't be so naive as to think Jordan wouldn't do the same to her. And to do so with some painted-up Sheila person…

Sheila?

Wait. Now she realized where she'd seen this woman before. She'd worked at Garrison Inc. as a receptionist. Her brother had even offered to send her over to help with paperwork while Brooke was on bed rest. How damn coincidental to find her brother's receptionist here.

Or was it?

A woman intimate with Jordan, yet she worked for Parker? At the least, it whispered of conflict of interest. At the worst, it screamed setup. Could this Sheila person be a corporate spy sent to scoop secrets from her family's business? Parker had said often enough that Jordan would do anything to win one over on the Garrisons.

Fury mingled with the disillusionment. She dashed her wrist across her cheek, swiping away foolish tears. She would be stronger than her mother.

However, for the first time, she sensed how deeply the years of betrayal must have cut Bonita.

"Brooke, hold on." Jordan's voice stroked over her a second before she felt the heat of him stopping behind her. "Nothing happened between me and Sheila McKay."

"Of course it didn't." She jabbed the button again. "I walked in."

Although who was to say she hadn't arrived at the tail end of a heated goodbye. She choked on the thought and the ball of tears at the back of her throat.

He sidestepped between her and the glowing down button. "Nothing was going to happen."

Right. "Has she or has she not been spying on my family's business while she worked for Parker? You promised always to be honest."

She hated the way he hesitated. But she wouldn't start crying again, not in front of him.

He pinched the bridge of his nose, eyes closing. From frustration? Or simply to gather his excuses?

Jordan looked at her again, his blue eyes appearing genuine—damn him. "In the *past,* Sheila and I saw each other. And yes, over the last few months she has brought information in an attempt to patch things up." He held up a finger to stop her from speaking. "But I have not slept with her since the first time you and I were together. Something changed for me that night. I didn't fully understand it then. I just knew no one interested me once I'd been with you."

His words rang true. Except...

"How do I know if I can trust you?"

He'd lied to her about the newspaper leak. He'd easily hid the truth about her mother's intervention. Although he'd made an eloquent case for why he'd tried.

Bottom line, she didn't want to be in a relationship full of secrets. Even if it cost her the family she'd just begun to dream about.

"Brooke..." He cupped the nape of her neck and rested his forehead against hers. "It's not good for you to upset yourself."

"No need to worry about me or the baby. The doctor gave me a clean bill of health today." She thanked God and all the saints for that. How could any woman have handled that scene in Jordan's office without some serious stress?

The sight of that viper's hands on him punched a hole clean through her.

"I'm so happy for you. Both of you. That's great news." A smile creased his handsome face. "Come on. Let's go home and talk about this."

Lord, she was tempted. His words sounded logical, his smile heartfelt. She wanted to believe him, which scared her most of all. But she couldn't cave to temptation. Besides, she had to tell Parker about the leak so he could make sure Sheila never set foot inside Garrison, Incorporated ever again.

Admitting that Parker had been right about Jordan all along hurt her pride almost as much as her heart. If only she could rest her head on Jordan's shoulder and give him a chance to persuade her.

The swoosh of the elevator doors opening cut through the silence, breaking her free of the momentary weakness that could lead her to lean into him. She shook off the allure of his looks, his charm, and whatever it was about him that seemed to hold her captive.

Despite what he thought about her seeming weakness around her family, she had always protected herself with space and distance, quietly insulating her heart from the jabs of those closest to her rather than fighting with angry words. She might not argue with him, but she would damn well think about this before sharing another ounce of herself with him.

Brooke inched away from him, pivoting back into the elevator. "I need time alone to mull this over."

"Fine." He held the doors open with flattened palms. "I'll stay out of your way at home tonight."

She knew if she walked into his house again she would end up in his bed. "I'm going to my condo. I can take care of myself now, remember? I've given you what you wanted these past few weeks with dates and getting to know each other. Now give me what I need. Space."

Brooke jabbed the close button. Thank goodness he took the hint and released the doors.

The elevator music swaddled her in claustrophobic memories of another time, another elevator, she and Jordan so hungry for each other.

As the chimes dinged with each passing floor, she realized her triumph would be short-lived. With her sister and Emilio's wedding only two days away, Brooke would see Jordan tomorrow night at the rehearsal dinner.

And the next day, she would face him as she came down the aisle in a church. Even though she wouldn't be the bride, the symbolism of the moment would be damn near unbearable with her heart already breaking.

Ten

Jordan popped a caviar canapé in his mouth at the reception, his mind still full of images of Brooke at the church service. She had never looked so beautiful to him as she did walking down the aisle this afternoon at the wedding.

Too bad the service had been for her sister and his brother. But as the maid of honor, Brooke had still been making her way toward him. Her Christmas red dress skimming her body. Hair swept up. A small bouquet shielding her stomach.

He'd barely noticed the bride in her beaded gown and veil—well, other than her train so long it could have clothed a couple of people. No. His attention had focused soundly on Brooke as she stole his breath then, and at the reception now.

He and Emilio had spent most of the evening before having a brother-to-brother chat after the bachelor party. They'd discussed the Sheila McKay debacle and the need to sit down with Parker soon to clear the air on that subject.

His sibling had also offered some words of wisdom about pursuing Brooke. Namely patience and honesty. Brooke was without a doubt the most sensitive of the Garrison clan.

Even at the reception on the Garrison estate, he couldn't take his eyes off her as she stood on the veranda talking to her sisters-in-law. They all wore the holiday crimson dresses, Brooke's higher waistband for her expanding stomach the only difference in the gowns. Their smaller rose bouquets lay discarded along the patio wall now that staged photos were complete. The Christmas themed wedding reminded him of the holiday he longed to spend with her. The gifts for her and the baby he'd wanted to share.

Reaching to snag another hors d'oeuvre from a passing waiter, Jordan nodded to Brandon as he strode by to claim his fiancée from the group of women. Jordan got good vibes from Brandon and Cassie after the way they'd played host and hostess to him. His memories of Brooke in the Bahamas kept him hopeful he could salvage some of the relationship they'd been working toward.

Except she was still keeping him on the deep freeze. No talking beyond polite exchanges in front of others. Blatant avoidance of any alone time.

She looked gorgeous, but tired. Moonbeams and the tiny white Christmas lights strung throughout the shrubbery accented the shadows under her eyes that no one would see except for somebody who knew her well.

Footsteps behind him shook him free. He turned to find Parker approaching, thrusting a drink his way. Given the dry ceremony, he knew the glass wouldn't contain more than sparkling water. Good, since he needed to keep his mind clear. A seemingly subdued Bonita Garrison had behaved so far during her day out of the rehab clinic. She'd even been polite in a brief—very brief—exchange with Cassie and Brandon.

But he wasn't taking anything for granted.

Jordan took the drink. "Thanks. I appreciate it."

Parker leaned back against the stone wall littered with poinsettia and rose arrangements. "I hear from Brooke that you and my receptionist Sheila McKay had a meeting this week."

Jordan tensed, unwilling to go another ten rounds with Parker at a family shindig. "Believe it or not, Emilio and I were just discussing the need to sit down and have a talk with you about Sheila." Aka the witch. He tried not to harbor such extreme ill will against a woman, but in Sheila's case, he would make an exception. "I thought Brooke would wait until after the wedding to tell you—to reduce chances of an uproar at the big event."

Parker tipped back his glass before answering, the sound of the tide tugging at the shore mingling with tunes from the band inside. "Brooke was pretty fired up when she talked to me. She wanted to make sure I knew so I could fire Sheila—pronto."

He tried to read Parker, but failed. The guy looked relaxed enough. Jordan stared into his drink. "Should I be wary of some kind of poison?"

A calculating grin split his adversary's face. "Maybe three weeks ago, but you're safe now. Unless, of course, you hurt Brooke."

"Your sister is tougher than you give her credit for. I'm pretty sure it's me who's the injured party this go-round." Jordan winced as he remembered Brooke's scowl when she'd caught the bride's bouquet just before Brittany and Emilio left to start their honeymoon in Greece. "All the same, I owe you an apology for the McKay incident."

Parker stuck out his hand. "Apology accepted."

Jordan stared at the hand suspiciously before shaking it slowly. "You're okay with things that easily?"

"Oh, I'm pissed." Parker grinned in contradiction to his words. "But I don't blame you. I'd have done the same in your shoes. It's business." His grin faded. "However, when it comes to family matters, I'm not nearly as forgiving. If you mess around on my sister, the next fist fight won't end well for you."

"Brooke is the only woman in my life, now and forever, if she'll have me." He stared through the crowd, searching for Brooke on the veranda, just to reassure himself she was still okay, but no sign of her. Just a few minglers, and Adam slow dancing on the beach with his wife Lauryn.

Jordan looked away from the happy couple wrapped up in a world of their own. He needed to clear the air with Brooke's brother, and to do that, he needed to be totally up-front. "Sheila McKay did come to me this week and offer more insider secrets in hopes of resuming our relationship."

"Since you're here telling me this, I guess that means you turned her down on the sex." Parker powered on, "So why haven't you talked to Brooke? You can convince her. Hell, I've witnessed your persuasive powers in the boardroom."

"Maybe... Except I can't help but think either she trusts me or she doesn't."

"She has a lot of reason *not* to trust people. Mother has wreaked hell on her over the years. For that matter, finding out Dad hadn't been honest with us about much of anything didn't help, either."

Jordan remembered the first night he'd spent with Brooke had been partly instigated by a swell of emotion she'd experienced after hearing her father's will. No doubt her ability to trust had been raked over serious coals that day.

He stared through the open French doors to where Bonita sat on a small settee looking suitably subdued as she spoke with a guest. Maybe there was still hope for some healing between Brooke and her mom at least. "I'm glad the intervention seems to have taken for your mom."

"Time will tell." Parker scooped his glass back for a long swig. "Okay, so I'm not saying you're the first man I would have chosen for my sister, but on second look, you're not all bad. You can hold your own in a fight."

Jordan certainly hadn't expected that. "Thank you."

"And I've been ticked off at you often enough to say with authority that you're a helluva businessman."

"Thanks, again." The guy was making a genuine effort and deserved something in return, for Brooke, for the baby and because he sensed that Parker could make an astute ally if they committed to working the same side of the fence. "Same to you on both accounts."

And damn, he meant it.

Glass in hand, Parker rattled the ice from side to side. "Seems as if this family linkup is a foregone conclusion, given Brittany's marriage and your baby."

"Apparently so." A year ago, he couldn't have imagined sharing such a civil conversation with Garrison. But a year ago, he'd also been too caught up in the thrill of the rat race to see the deceit in Sheila McKay.

"I've been doing some life review stuff lately, thanks to all those family support meetings we're having to go to with Mom's treatment." The ice clinking stopped. "I think it's time you and I laid down the arms and joined forces."

Holy crap. Garrison was actually suggesting… "A merger between Jefferies Brothers and Garrison, Incorporated."

Could it ever work? Hell, maybe there could be some benefits. Benefits cagey Parker was already seeing.

"It would take negotiating, but yes, basically."

Jordan let his brain wrap around the notion of blending the two corporations, abandoning the competition that had consumed them both for so many years.

A competition that had led him to keep his distance from Brooke in spite of his attraction to her the first time she'd glided through his radar.

The notion had serious merits and incredible possibilities. For that matter, it might create a lot more peace on the home front. Of course, he couldn't make that kind of business move without having Emilio on board. Not that he could see his brother arguing, not since his marriage to Brittany. "I'll have to confer with Emilio since we're partners in the holding, but I'm more than intrigued by your offer."

Parker relaxed his stance, his eyes glinting with a business acumen and excitement. "Staking a monopoly on the hotel and entertainment segment for this area would make you and me happy."

Jordan could feel himself warming to the notion,

the possibility of what they could accomplish with their combined drives. "For just South Beach? You think small, Garrison."

Parker's laughter rumbled free and they clinked their glasses together with the promise of a greater business celebration yet to come.

If only his problems with Brooke could be so easily negotiated and resolved. To hell with waiting for her to figure this out on her own. He could at least talk to her.

Jordan searched the crowd again to find her, tell her. Convince her. Except the bridesmaids had all scattered, their gathering spot now occupied by Brandon and Cassie sitting on the stone railing sharing a single plate of food.

He scanned the beach where Adam and Lauryn still danced. Then glanced over at the open French doors to the foyer where the band played, Stephen and his wife, Megan, making the most of the music, as well.

He looked through the window to the dining area with all the food. Bonita was helping her granddaughter, Jade, tuck a napkin in her shirt to protect her flower girl dress from her snack.

Still no sign of Brooke.

"You're right, Garrison. I need to make things right with Brooke. I don't want more time to pass with her so upset, especially without reason." He couldn't see her anyplace. "I have to speak with her."

"She just left." Anna spoke, having somehow snuck up behind the men undetected. She slipped an arm around her husband's waist. "Don't bother asking where she's gone. I swore not to tell."

She'd left? Hidden was more like it. "So you do know."

Anna gauged him through narrowed eyes. "As much as I would like to watch you squirm a little — I do still owe you for that sucker punch to my husband's gut—I've also seen how miserable my sister-in-law is without you."

And he couldn't even take pleasure from that because he hated to think of Brooke unhappy. "Then where the hell is she?"

Anna bit her lip, but hesitated only a moment.

"Think—" she tapped her forehead with a manicured nail "—and you can figure it out. If she wants to run from you, where would she go to get her head together?"

His mind churned with what he knew about her, what he'd learned during their intensely compacted time together. The answer took shape. "She would go to family. But everyone is here except the bride and groom." He scanned the family decked out in gowns and tuxedos. His gaze hooked on Cassie. Her sister. A confidante—who would be flying home in the morning. "She's going to Cassie's place?"

Anna stayed silent, but smiled slightly.

Parker's grin, however, was full-out. "I know that look on my wife's face, Jefferies, and you're on the right track."

Okay, thank God. He just had to find her before

she made it to the airport. "So there's time to stop her before she joins up with Cassie and Brandon to fly out."

Anna frowned a definite no, apparently still bent on not speaking on the subject.

"Why would she leave ahead of them—"

"God," Anna blurted, "for a smart guy, you're really not thinking like your corporate shark self today. You must actually be in love. It wreaks havoc with a guy's brain if he doesn't get things straightened out. She's taking the family yacht to the Bahamas so she'll get there after Cassie returns. And don't start hollering about her health. She hired a nurse to accompany her, just to be safe."

He exhaled his relief at having found her and, thank God, that she had the foresight to watch over herself and the baby, even during a short trip to the Bahamas.

Then the rest of Anna's words penetrated his thoughts.

In love?

In love.

Damn straight. He loved Brooke Garrison. Not just because she carried his child, but because all other women faded around her. She was it for him. His chance to have what his parents shared, and he didn't want to waste another second apart from her.

Now he just needed to convince Brooke he wasn't a scumbag so he could tell her how damn much he loved her.

* * *

Brooke lounged on one of the yacht's deck chairs, searching the starlit night for answers to the confusion swirling inside her. A gust of wind rolling in off the ocean sent her clutching her lightweight sweater closed over the bridesmaid gown she still wore.

She probably should have just gone back to her place, but all the love and sentimentality of the wedding had left her so weepy, she needed to get away. Far away, before she puddled into a serious crying jag. Thank goodness she'd been able to hire a nurse to come along on such short notice, the only way her sisters and sisters-in-law would help her leave.

In the middle of the swirl of aching feelings, a memory of spending time with her father on their yacht brought her an unexpected comfort. Right now, she appreciated the total quiet here and she needed that utter peace for her baby after the emotional hubbub of most of her pregnancy. Here in the quiet, she could sense her father's presence, could almost hear his apology. He hadn't been perfect, but he had been there for her as best he knew how. She could see that now as she viewed the world in a way that involved less extremes and more middle ground.

The past couple of days since seeing Jordan with Sheila McKay had been hell. She missed him more than she could have imagined. How could he have worked his way so completely into her life in such a short time?

Or had this been a long time coming?

She wanted to trust his explanation about the incident with Sheila. Her instincts shouted that he'd told her the truth. But her heart wanted a clear sign that her love was reciprocated.

Yes, she loved Jordan Jefferies. She couldn't deny it any longer. Maybe in some corner of her heart she'd always known but had been too afraid of the family fallout to pursue the possibility. She wasn't afraid of her family's disapproval anymore.

She was, however, afraid of making a mistake, for her own sake and that of her baby. How would she ever know for certain?

Her gaze shifted from the stars—Orion wasn't offering up any answers anyhow—down to the opaque ocean. A dim light chopped through the darkness, another late-night boater. The gently lapping waves might not have solutions either, but at least the rhythmic sound lulled her at a time she desperately needed ease from the agitation.

The drone of the other boat grew louder, the beam closer. The sleek craft took shape, smaller than she'd expected. Who used a ski boat this late at night? A hint of anxiousness stirred in her gut. She started to rise and alert the captain, when one of the crew came out onto her deck.

"The captain said to let you know we have company. But no worries, ma'am. The boat's one of ours. There's a family member on board."

"Thank you for the update." Family?

Brooke rose from the chair and walked toward

the metal railing, curious. Concerned. Her relatives should all be at the wedding. Jordan didn't know where she was. She'd only told the girls because she'd thought someone should be aware...

The ski boat drew nearer, two towering males becoming visible, a pair of tall figures in tuxedos standing. The craft drew up alongside. She backed a step.

Parker *and* Jordan.

Her heart did a quick flip-flop much like the fish plopping in the ocean. She should have known Jordan would find out and follow her. Especially after she'd turned him away. And somehow he'd won her brother over to his side. Which led him here.

Someone had ratted her out. Now she faced not only Jordan but her meddling control-freak brother, as well. Still, her pulse picked up speed at the sight of Jordan, who'd come all this way for her.

She gripped the rail and shouted, "Parker Garrison, you traitor. You're officially out of my will."

Her brother slowed back the engine as the boat neared the yacht. "You've been saying that since you were six and I kicked over your sand castle."

Yet another instance when her family had tried to dictate her life to her.

She'd put a lot of time and dreams into that sand castle. All she'd ever wanted was a happily-ever-after of her own and damned if she would let her brother mess that up, even if he meant well. She'd had enough of putting her own needs on the back burner just to keep the peace. Making the right decision about Jordan was too important for her and her child. "I meant it then, Parker, and I really mean it now. Don't interfere in my life."

"I think you should hear Jefferies out."

"*You* think?" Her fingers clenched around the railing, and it was all she could do not to stamp her foot in frustration. "What gives you the right to decide?"

Jordan stopped Parker with a hand to his arm. "She's correct. She makes the decision as to whether I go or stay." With an agile leap, he stepped up and out onto the bow of the ski boat, his balance steady as the craft rocked beneath him. "You know that we have to talk sometime. But I won't come on board unless you want me to."

"I don't want you to." Her lips lied even as her heart cried out for her to give him a chance. "I need time to think."

"Fair enough. I'll go back."

Her next argument stalled in her mouth. He was giving up that easily? Disappointment melted through her veins…until she realized he hadn't moved. She knew. He was waiting for her to tell him flat out to go. Somehow she couldn't force those words past her lips.

She blinked against the whipping ocean wind plastering her bridesmaid dress to her body. Those weren't tears of hope stinging her eyes, damn it.

Okay, maybe they were. She could at least listen to what he had to say as long as he stayed off the yacht and on the bow.

Sea spray splashed up across Jordan's shoes, but his feet stayed planted, his attention focused solely on her. "While you're thinking, I want you to consider the fact that I love you."

Drat, there went her heart with the flip-flopping again. But she still needed her sign that she could believe those beautiful words she'd been longing to here.

"I love you, Brooke Garrison, and no matter what happens between us, I want you to have this." He held out his hand with a small jewelry box in his palm. The sort of little velvet box that held a ring.

He lowered his hand as if to toss the box up to her.

"Wait!" she shouted. "Don't you dare throw that at me. What if you miss?"

"I won't," he said with such assurance she almost smiled at his predictable arrogance.

"How about you hold on to it while you keep talking." She fisted both hands to resist the temptation to motion him up onto the yacht and say to hell with signs. He'd said he loved her, and she wanted his diamond on her finger like the ones all the other women in her family now possessed. Even though she always could have afforded whatever gems she pleased, she found herself craving the emotional commitment that came with this particular stone.

Caution and pride overrode impulse to take what she wanted without weighing the cost.

"I can't make you believe me." Moonbeams glinted on his blond hair, casting shadows along the serious lines of his face, her hunky charmer completely somber. "That trust has to come from you. I'm willing to wait as long as it takes for you to believe me."

Jordan opened the box. Starlight sparked off the ohmigod-huge diamond inside.

"So you're proposing—again." Did he really think she could be bought with a big rock? A beautiful big rock held by the man she loved.

If this were real, what a memory it would make, her handsome man in a tuxedo proposing from the bow of a boat. All the practical, cautious parts of her cried out for the beautiful romanticism of it to be real.

He shook his head. "No, I'm not going to ask you to marry me again, unless that's what you want." Jordan extended his hand, his feet so sure against the jostling waves that could too easily send the priceless gem to the bottom of the bay. "I am, however, asking you to wear my mom's ring."

His mother's? Was this a trick? "That's an engagement ring."

"Wear it on your right hand if you want." His voice carried strong and clear on the night breeze whipping over the water. "I've been saving this to give the one woman for me. No matter what you decide, this ring could only belong to you."

Wow. Her sign.

How funny that she'd been searching for a big symbol for why she could trust him, and the answer came to her in a way she'd never expected.

The sentimentality of his ring touched her heart so much more than anything he could have bought. He could *purchase* anything. But this was like the time he'd chosen the painting for her. He understood her, the essence of her and what she would want. He knew her heart.

And as an added bonus, he'd even said all those humbling words in front of her brother.

She saw the two men, side by side, both so self-assured, successful and yes, more than a little arrogant. But men a woman could count on. Men who were willing to lay it on the line for a woman—one woman.

Jordan was a man to trust. She knew it now without question.

He'd won his chance to stay, a chance to tell her more about why he loved her.

She stepped back from the rail and crooked her finger at him. "Okay, then. Come aboard and we'll talk."

A deep smile creased his face, but she could swear she also saw relief in his starlit blue eyes.

Jordan climbed the ladder to board and she got a close-up look at the ring—an emerald-cut diamond with tapered baguettes. Beautiful for its sentimentality even more than the magnificence of the cut and size. Victoria's ring had been worn with a love that lasted all her days.

A whistle sounded from the ski boat, from Parker. "Hello? So, Brooke? Do I go or stick around?"

She stared at the diamond, his mother's ring. She'd known about Jordan for a long time, thanks to gossip and common business dealings. He was the last man to show a softer side to anyone. Yet, he'd done so here, tonight. And now she knew she was woman enough to stand up to him during those times his stubbornness got the best of him.

"Parker?"

"Yeah, kid?"

"You're back in the will." He winked. "Be happy."

The engine on the ski boat gurgled to life again as her brother backed the craft, then roared away into the night.

Leaving her alone on the deck with Jordan.

Jordan tipped her face up to his. "Is this a yes or a no?"

The yes already sang inside her, begging to be set free, but goodness, she deserved to revel in this moment. "Could you repeat what you said out there?"

She expected him to grin that arrogant smile of self-assurance. She'd all but told him he'd won, after all.

Instead, his face stayed sober. Intense. "I love you, Brooke. Not because you're carrying my child, although Lord knows that stirs something inside me I never could have imagined. I love you because you're you. And when I'm around you, I'm a better me. Together, I believe we can build one helluva lifetime."

He'd made his case well.

Joy rushed through her as strong as any tide tugging the yacht. "I guess we're a very lucky couple, because I happen to love you, too."

She rested her hands on his chest. A gust of breath rocked through him at just her touch. She understood the feeling well. Brooke arched up to meet his kiss, his mouth warm and wonderful and blessedly familiar against hers. A yearning, equally as familiar and growing stronger every day, began to build inside her. A longing they would be able to fulfill, thanks to her doctor's okay.

She looped her arms around his neck to deepen their kiss—

A tiny foot booted inside her. Hard. Hard enough so that Jordan jerked back in surprise.

He shook his head as if to clear his thoughts. "Wow, I guess I should be used to that now, but it's still so damn amazing."

She grasped his hand to flatten along their child. "I totally agree."

They stood together for—well, she lost track of the time until he lifted her hand, the ring magically appearing in his other hand.

"Brooke, will you marry me?"

He'd asked. Not demanded. She hadn't expected two signs in one night. But then she'd never expected to fall so utterly in love with Jordan Jefferies.

She extended her fingers. "Yes, I will marry you, and love you and share my life with you. Together."

His eyes closed briefly and she understood the feeling. She knew him now as well as he knew her.

His eyes blinked back open and he slid the ring onto her finger, sealing its placement with a kiss to her hand. Then he let out a shout that sent her laughing just as he scooped her into his arms again. He took her place in the lounger, cradling her in his lap.

She'd expected he would take her below deck, but at the moment he seemed to be more interested in holding her, kissing her, stroking her and drawing out the moment in a way she would cherish all her life.

Especially since she knew they *would* eventually end up below deck.

Finally, he pulled back, his thumb fiddling with the ring on her finger. "If you prefer something of your own choosing for an engagement, we can pick it out together. I won't be offended if you wear this on your right hand."

She shook her head, lifting her hand so the moonlight could catch the facets of the cut. "It's perfect."

"You're sure? You really don't want to go jewelry shopping?"

"You silly man." She clasped his face in both hands, his five o'clock shadow rasping tantalizingly along her skin. "We both have enough money to buy anything we want. This ring is about things so much more important than money. Sentiment. Family. Love."

He stroked his knuckles down her cheek, his eyes shining with a hint of awe and a lot of love. "You really do trust me, then."

"This ring and the fact that you knew to choose it for me tells me everything I need to know."

His killer, gorgeous smile returned. "And to think I almost screwed up by spending a mint."

"You can still do that if you really want."

His laugh rumbled against her chest and she enjoyed the chance to laugh along with him with ease, secure in their love.

"How did you manage to get this ring and still find me so quickly? I haven't been gone long so you must have set out in the ski boat right away."

He stayed silent and the answer slowly dawned on her. "You've been carrying this set around? For how long?"

"Since the day I left your office, right after you turned me down the first time I asked."

And to think the sentiment, his understanding of family, and yes, even the seeds of love had been there right from the start if only she'd been able to see through her own fears. "I guess I'm the one who's been silly."

"Not at all. You're a wise one, Brooke Garrison. It's good we're getting this right."

"It's going to stick. This marriage idea. The way we love each other."

"Damn straight. And it's only going to get better." He eased up from the lounger, keeping her in his arms as he turned toward the stairway leading below deck. "Merry Christmas, beautiful."

She nipped his bristly jaw with a kiss. "Merry Christmas, to both of us."

Epilogue

He'd seen her many times. He'd always wanted her.

Tonight, once her family finished their meal, he would have her.

Jordan covered Brooke's cool, slim fingers tucked in the corner of his arm as they sat together at the reception dinner after their wedding. Eager to make things official, they'd scheduled the nuptials for the first weekend after Emilio and Brittany's return from their European honeymoon.

The January ceremony had been a small family affair at a chapel on the beach in the Bahamas. They'd had enough with media frenzies and gratefully accepted Cassie's generous offer to host the private reception. A lavish event, the house full of candles, flowers, food—and family.

He'd never seen Brooke look more beautiful than at their ceremony, with the Bahamas sunset streaming across her creamy skin and her golden yellow dress. The glow had glinted highlights on her dark hair, swept back in a twist—with a lone strand slithering free, of course.

He stared around the table of smiling faces and couldn't help but contrast this happy gathering with the tense confrontation the first time he'd eaten with her relatives last month.

Tonight, her two sisters wore their green bridesmaid gowns, his groomsmen in tuxedos. He'd chosen his brother and his new business partner, Parker, surprising himself with the decision as well as the oldest Garrison offspring.

Brooke squeezed Jordan's arm, smiling and nodding in the direction of her brother as steel drum music wafted softly in the distance. "I can't believe you two are speaking, much less that Jefferies Brothers and Garrison, Incorporated are officially merging. And to have Parker in the wedding, too, I'm thrilled—and still a little stunned."

Jordan set aside his fork with a clink against china. "It was worth it to see the shock on his face. It's not often anyone can render that guy speechless."

Parked arched a brow as he silently finished the last of his Bahamian rock lobster.

Anna stroked her husband's shoulder. "No brawls today, dear."

"Don't worry." Parker captured his wife's wrist to kiss her palm. "I wouldn't risk upsetting you or my sister in your delicate conditions."

Anna rolled her eyes, eyes that held a definite twinkle of excitement as she smoothed both hands over her expanding waistline. "There's nothing delicate about me right now."

"You're all the more gorgeous." Parker placed his hand over hers on her stomach and directed his words to her pregnant swell. "Right, John?"

Jordan took in the spontaneous family moment with an inward grin. Well, hell, the guy had a softer side after all. And what a sign of how far they'd all come in a month for Parker to name his child after the deceased patriarch who'd stirred so much turmoil for his children.

For that matter, having a serenely sober Bonita sit at the same table with Cassie was an event even Jordan had doubted could happen. Bonita had completed her four-week program at the rehab clinic and now attended A.A. meetings at least every other day. Brooke's mother had even approached them with her hopes to stay sober and be a healthy grandmother to her grandchildren. She radiated a quiet determination that boded well for her *and* her family.

Anna broke the long, affectionate look with her husband and shifted her attention to Brooke. "Have you two chosen a name for your little guy?"

Jordan slid an arm around his wife's shoulders. *Wife.* Damn, that had an amazing ring to it. "I think I have the perfect name picked out, but I'll need to run it past Brooke first."

No more unilateral decisions when it came to their future. He'd found a real partner in this quietly determined woman who'd been smart enough to make them explore their feelings for each other before committing.

She elbowed him gently in the side. "About the name thing, I'm not going to agree with Uncle Fester no matter how nicely you ask."

"I think you'll like this one better. We can talk later." He reached to the sprawling centerpiece and pulled an orchid free. Gently, he tucked the flower behind her ear, wondering if she recalled their time here together when he'd teased her naked flesh with a similar blossom.

From the warming of her brown eyes, she most definitely remembered.

Brooke tipped her face to kiss him while the family applauded. The cheers and clapping faded and Brooke eased back.

Their kiss may have been short but it was powerful. His body heated in response to her unspoken promise of the pleasure they would enjoy once they reached the yacht, anchored in the harbor. He stared into her eyes, tempted to leave now, until chuckles from around the table pulled him back to the moment.

Blushing, Brooke turned to Cassie next to her. "Thank you so much for arranging such a lovely dinner—" She stopped abruptly and clasped her half sister's wrist. "Hey, is that a wedding band I see along with the engagement ring?"

Cassie exchanged an intimate grin with her fiancé—or rather apparently her former fiancé. "Brandon and I eloped. We had a secret wedding two weeks ago. We just got back from our honeymoon."

Squealing, Brooke threw her arms around her sister as Brittany rushed from her chair to join in the hug. The genuine emotion between all three women couldn't be missed. In spite of the havoc John Garrison had brought to them, they'd managed to forge a bond and find peace.

Brooke finally pulled back to reclaim her chair. "Why didn't you tell us?"

Brandon clasped Cassie's hand in his. "We didn't want to take away from your special day."

"Take away?" Brooke waved aside the notion. "This only adds to the joy. I'm so happy for both of you. This should be a double reception. Right, Jordan?"

"Absolutely. Congratulations!" Jordan lifted his glass of sparkling water to toast the new couple. "To Brandon and Cassie."

Brandon lifted his crystal glass, as well. "And to Jordan and Brooke."

Little Jade jumped up to stand on her chair. "And to my new baby brother or sister on the way!"

Laughing, Stephen wrapped an arm around his blushing wife, Megan, while patting Jade on the shoulder.

After everyone replaced their drinks and the catering staff began clearing away the china, Cassie led the way to the three-tiered wedding cake being served outside. The warm night and scent of the ocean beckoned. Beyond the sets of French doors, torches on the beach led down to the water.

"Jordan, wait just a moment." Brooke stopped him just shy of the open door and tugged him behind a decorative potted palm.

He braced a hand on her back. "Is everything all right?"

"Totally." She leaned forward, her body brushing his. "I couldn't have asked for a more wonderful wedding—and husband."

He cupped her face for a kiss, this one far longer than the one at the table as he made the most of even this brief private time together. A prelude to more they would enjoy soon. Not soon enough.

The sweet sweep of her tongue teased his senses along with the scent of the flower in her hair.

She nipped his bottom lip as her hand slid inside his tuxedo jacket. "So tell me more about your idea for a baby name. I'm too curious to wait."

"I like it when you're impatient." He skimmed his knuckles along the side of her breast before addressing her question. "What about naming our son Garrison?"

Jordan waited for her verdict while Brooke's eyes took on that soft brown mulling expression. God, he loved how he understood her.

"Garrison Jefferies." Brooke tested the combination, a smile slowly spreading over her face. "I like it, I love it. I love *you*."

He gathered her close again, a pleasure he looked forward to pursuing further throughout their honeymoon. Thanks to Brooke, he'd learned the importance of enjoying life along the way. Already, he could imagine making a lifetime of memories, filling their house with photographs, turning his place into their home. "I love you, too, beautiful." He curved a hand over their growing child. "And you, as well, Garrison Jefferies."

Garrison Jefferies—now that it was official, their child's name settled inside him with a rightness as special as the woman in his arms waiting to share wedding cake with all their relatives.

And wasn't that the biggest surprise of all? Especially to a man used to being ahead of the curve on everything. He'd known the name choice offered a nice symbol of their combined empires.

He'd just hadn't realized how damn amazing it would be to join the Garrisons and Jefferies into one family.

* * * * *

Turn the page for a sneak preview
of the first book in the new miniseries
DIAMONDS DOWN UNDER
From Silhouette Desire®
VOWS & A VENGEFUL GROOM
By Bronwyn Jameson

Available January 2008
(SD #1843)

Silhouette Desire®
Always Powerful, Passionate and Provocative

Kimberley Blackstone didn't notice the waiting horde of media until it was too late. Flashbulbs exploded around her like a New Year's light show. She skidded to a halt, so abruptly her trailing suitcase all but overtook her.

This had to be a case of mistaken identity. Surely. Kimberley hadn't been on the paparazzi hit list for close to a decade, not since she'd estranged herself from her billionaire father and his headline-hungry diamond business.

But no, it was *her* name they called. *Her* face was the focus of a swarm of lenses that circled her like avid hornets. Her heart started to pound with fear-fueled adrenaline.

What did they want?

What was going on?

With a rising sense of bewilderment she scanned the crowd for a clue, and her gaze fastened on a tall, leonine figure forcing his way to the front. A tall, familiar figure. Her head came up in stunned recognition, and their gazes collided across the sea of heads before the cameras erupted with another barrage of flashes, this time right in her exposed face.

Blinded by the flashbulbs—and by the shock of that momentary eye-meet—Kimberley didn't realize his intent until he'd forged his way to her side, possibly by the sheer strength of his personality. She felt his arm wrap around her shoulder, pulling her into the protective shelter of his body, allowing her no time to object. No chance to lift her hands to ward him off.

In the space of a hastily drawn breath, she found herself plastered knee-to-nose against six feet two inches of hard-bodied male.

Ric Perrini.

Her lover for ten torrid weeks, her husband for ten tumultuous days.

Her ex for ten tranquil years.

After all this time, he should not have felt so familiar but, oh dear, he did. She knew the scent of that body and its lean, muscular strength. She knew its heat and its slick power and every response it could draw from hers.

She also recognized the ease with which he'd

taken control of the moment and the decisiveness of his deep voice when it rumbled close to her ear. "I have a car waiting outside. Is this your only luggage?"

Kimberley nodded. "I assume you will tell me," she said tightly, "what this welcome party is all about."

"Not while the welcome party is within earshot. No."

Barking a request for the cameramen to stand aside, Perrini took her hand and pulled her into step with his ground-eating stride. Kimberley let him, because he was right, damn his arrogant, Italian-suited hide. Despite the speed with which he whisked her across the airport terminal, she could almost feel the hot breath of the pursuing media on her back.

This was neither the time nor the place for explanations. Inside his car, however, she would get answers.

Now that the initial shock had been blown away— by the haste of their retreat, by the heat of her gathering indignation, by the rush of adrenaline fired by Perrini's presence and the looming verbal battle— her brain was starting to tick over. This had to be her father's doing. And if it was a Howard Blackstone publicity ploy, then it had to be about Blackstone Diamonds, the company that ruled his life.

The knowledge made her chest tighten with a familiar ache of disillusionment.

She'd known her father would be flying in from Sydney for today's opening of the newest in his chain of exclusive, high-end jewelry boutiques. The opulent shopfront sat adjacent to the rival business where Kimberley worked. No coincidence, she thought bitterly, just as it was no coincidence that Ric Perrini was here in Auckland ushering her to his car.

Perrini was Howard Blackstone's right-hand man, second in command at Blackstone Diamonds, a legacy of his short-lived marriage to the boss's daughter. No doubt her father had sent him to fetch her; the question was *why?*

* * * * *

*Get swept away down under with the glitz
and glamour of the Blackstone empire as
Kimberley tries to determine the real
reason behind her "reunion" with Ric....*

Look for
VOWS & A VENGEFUL GROOM
By Bronwyn Jameson
In stores January 2008

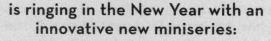

nocturne™

Jachin Black always knew he was an outcast.
Not only was he a vampire, he was a vampire
banished from the Sanguinas society. Jachin, forced
to survive among mortals, is determined to buy
his way back into the clan one day.

Ariel Swanson, debut author of a vampire novel, could
be the ticket he needs to get revenge and take his
rightful place among the Sanguinas again. However,
the unsuspecting mortal woman has no idea of the
dark and sensual path she will be forced to travel.

Look for

RESURRECTION: THE BEGINNING

by

PATRICE MICHELLE

Available January 2008 wherever you buy books.

REQUEST YOUR FREE BOOKS!

2 FREE NOVELS PLUS 2 FREE GIFTS!

Silhouette®

Desire®

Passionate, Powerful, Provocative!

YES! Please send me 2 FREE Silhouette Desire® novels and my 2 FREE gifts. After receiving them, if I don't wish to receive any more books, I can return the shipping statement marked "cancel." If I don't cancel, I will receive 6 brand-new novels every month and be billed just $3.80 per book in the U.S., or $4.47 per book in Canada, plus 25¢ shipping and handling per book and applicable taxes, if any*. That's a savings of almost 15% off the cover price! I understand that accepting the 2 free books and gifts places me under no obligation to buy anything. I can always return a shipment and cancel at any time. Even if I never buy another book from Silhouette, the two free books and gifts are mine to keep forever.

225 SDN EEXJ   326 SDN EEXU

Name	(PLEASE PRINT)
Address	Apt.
City	State/Prov.	Zip/Postal Code

Signature (if under 18, a parent or guardian must sign)

Mail to the **Silhouette Reader Service™:**
IN U.S.A.: P.O. Box 1867, Buffalo, NY 14240-1867
IN CANADA: P.O. Box 609, Fort Erie, Ontario L2A 5X3

Not valid to current Silhouette Desire subscribers.

Want to try two free books from another line?
Call 1-800-873-8635 or visit www.morefreebooks.com.

* Terms and prices subject to change without notice. NY residents add applicable sales tax. Canadian residents will be charged applicable provincial taxes and GST. This offer is limited to one order per household. All orders subject to approval. Credit or debit balances in a customer's account(s) may be offset by any other outstanding balance owed by or to the customer. Please allow 4 to 6 weeks for delivery.

Your Privacy: Silhouette is committed to protecting your privacy. Our Privacy Policy is available online at www.eHarlequin.com or upon request from the Reader Service. From time to time we make our lists of customers available to reputable firms who may have a product or service of interest to you. If you would prefer we not share your name and address, please check here. ☐

SDES07